Party Girl Nurse's
Journey

Party Girl Nurse's Journey

Victoria Godwin

Library of Congress Control Number:		2016906497
ISBN:	Hardcover	978-1-5144-8743-3
	Softcover	978-1-5144-8742-6
	eBook	978-1-5144-8741-9

Print information available on the last page.

Rev. date: 07/26/2016

To order additional copies of this book, contact:
Xlibris
1-888-795-4274
www.Xlibris.com
Orders@Xlibris.com
733932

Contents

Preface ix

Roots...1

The Big Move Begins 6

Teen Times 10

Graduation and College-Bound..15

Rocky Mountain Adventures...22

Internship and Europe...33

Nursing School Begins 42

Life While Married to Landon 49

Starting Over Again...57

The Beginning of My Journey with Ted 66

Our Big Move for Medical School..72

Ted's Residency 76

Life in the Little City 82

The Beginning of the Drug World 90

The Realization of the Big Betrayal 102

The Illness...110

Life after Ted...122

Life with Just the Girls at Home..134

My First Heart Fling after Ted 140

Mark's Fall 144

The Assisted-Living Experience 150

Disappointment, Forgiveness, and Saying Good-Bye 154

Our Family Journeys Continue 158

To my children, who have helped me grow up and be a more responsible person. We have gone through hell and back as a family, and God has kept us safe through it all.

To my parents, who were always outstanding examples of how parents should be.

Preface

It was prophesied that I would write this book while I was getting a prayer request on a prayer line on the phone. It came as a complete surprise to me and to the woman I was talking to. She said it so confidently, yet she sounded just as astonished as I was.

I had told one of my patients in the nursing home I worked at that I was working on this book. He said he wanted to read it, but I told him I didn't want him to know how bad I had been when I was younger. He just laughed. Now he will get the chance to read it in heaven. Enjoy.

Roots

HE WAS BORN A TWO-POUND TWIN, THREE minutes behind his three-and-a-half-pound twin sister. Back then there were no incubators or neonatal intensive care units, which came with the benefits of modern medical technology. They put him in a shoe box instead. A miracle happened, and both Mac and Mara healthfully thrived.

They were both very different from each other. Mara was dark haired, had brown eyes, and was very feisty and mischievous. Mac was white haired, had blue eyes, and was very mellow and good-natured. He never got into trouble, unless his sister, Mara, pulled him into it. He said there was no other bond like the bond of twins. He said it was like they knew each other's thoughts.

Mara and Mac were the youngest of three other siblings. It was the 1920s, and their father was the principal of a small southern town high school. Their mom, my grandmother Maggie, was an elementary school teacher.

They had a kind, soft-spoken black man who worked for them around the house, and when the twins were born, he asked if he could stay as part of the family and take care of them. To this day, I think Uncle Joe—as they called him—helped influence Mac to be the kind, mellow man whom he grew up to be.

My grandparents also had a jovial, always smiling black cook, who made the best typical southern cuisine. Her name was Annie; and she made the best corn bread, collards, and fried chicken that any restaurant could boast about. Grandma Maggie made biscuits that melted in your mouth. Then we had ambrosia, a dessert made from fruit and coconut.

Near the dining room, my grandma Maggie had several cages of finches, and they would sing while we ate our meals. She also had cats and kittens on the back porch that we loved to play with.

It was a Christmas tradition for us to visit my grandparents as we were growing up. The drive seemed long, but my mom played games with us that made the time seem to go by faster.

My dad, Mac, and his siblings were all very different from one another. He had a sister who was somewhat of a rebel. She was an art teacher in New York City and illustrated books. She rode a motorcycle all over the United States and never married.

The other middle sister was a nurse and ended up marrying a doctor, and they moved to California. They lived in a beautiful ranch-style house on top of a mountain with scenic big redwood trees all the way up their driveway. I used to love to visit them because they also had four gorgeous sons. Too bad they were my cousins.

I had a slight crush on my father's older brother, John. He had a slow southern drawl and big brown eyes. He called me his cupcake. He worked for a research company and invented a sweetener.

We were such a loving Christian family, and we all loved one another unconditionally. I thought everyone was like us.

My dad ended up going to medical school, graduating second in his class. He said he would have graduated first, but he admitted he played a little bit too much toward the end of school. He also played football even though he was smaller, but he was very strong. He even made his own weights out of cement before weight lifting was popular.

He was the ship doctor aboard a destroyer as chief medical officer during WWII in the South Pacific and retired as a commander. Later, he was honored at a special ceremony for his positive influence on his shipmates' lives.

God was definitely with Mac one day during "mess call." Mac was busy attending to one of the patients on the ship, so he switched shifts with one of the other men. That man was killed that day while eating lunch in the exact seat that Mac was supposed to be sitting in. He felt terrible about it, but he had no way of knowing what was about to happen.

On a destroyer, you would never know when you were going to be hit or had to destroy another ship. They were large armored warships with a main battery consisting of heavy-caliber guns. When they went off, they were very loud, and that was the main contributing factor to why my dad was so hard of hearing in his later years.

Mac had many stories about his time on the ship. He had to do an appendectomy in the middle of a storm, with the ship moving up and down from the heavy waves. Another time, one of the men, who was a recruit, stated that he was a sleepwalker and felt like being on a ship was not a good idea for him. Mac examined him and confirmed it, but since many young men were trying to get out of going out to sea, particularly on a destroyer, the higher officials didn't believe him. Mac was upset with them, but when they couldn't find the young man, they knew he was telling the truth. He had sleepwalked right off the ship. Hopefully, the recruiters had somewhat of a guilty conscience.

Everyone loved Mac. He treated everyone the same, whether they were ship cleaners or an officer. He was just a kind man who honestly cared about others. He was the epitome of what a doctor should be.

My mom, Fran, was born twenty years after her three sisters. She said she felt like she was an only child with four mothers. She was raised on a small country farm in the South and was bored, except when several cute boys down the road could play with her.

Fran's sisters had all married and moved away. Two of them were nurses. They still lived in Virginia but not close enough for frequent visits. Fran always looked older than her age. She had developed physically early, so everyone thought she was older. Also, being like an only child made her act older and not quite as childish as others who had siblings to play with. Her mom and dad tended to spoil her also.

At the age of seventeen, Fran's mom, my grandmother, got cancer. Fran basically took care of her mother most of the time. Nurses would come in and help and tell her what to do when they weren't there. It was totally overwhelming for Fran. The nurses had instructed her to give her mom morphine to help ease the pain. It was exasperating for Fran to be the one to decide whether to give her the morphine or not, depending on her pain. She had not been trained to be a nurse, and watching her mom dying in front of her eyes was more than she could bear.

Her two sisters who were nurses came to help when they realized how difficult the situation was. This relieved Fran's anxiety somewhat, but she never got over feeling guilty that she had perhaps given her mother too much morphine. I told her later, once I was part of her life, that professional nurses did that now as part of a service for cancer patients, and they even have morphine pumps that the patient or the nurse could keep beside them at all times. I hoped that this eased her mind.

Fran's dad ended up marrying one of the nurses who helped take care of her mom. For some reason, Fran was very angry with her dad for doing that. I guess she felt betrayed in a way. Losing your mom at eighteen years old was difficult enough, but having her quickly replaced by a stepmom was too much for her. I didn't know all the details, but I only met him once.

After the war, Mac was a doctor at a big teaching hospital in Virginia. Fran was working there as a radiology tech. She had lied about her age so she could work there, and back then they needed all the help they could get. She always looked older with her big boobs and very fit figure. She was pretty with long honey-colored hair.

One day, she was transporting a patient from his wheelchair and trying to get him back into bed when he started having a seizure. She looked around for a nurse to help her, but she couldn't find one. She started getting anxious, so she asked the first person she saw in a white coat to help her. She didn't want to leave the patient alone, so she yelled out, "Help! I need somebody to help me!"

There was a nice-looking young man in a white coat passing by the door who heard her yelling out. He immediately knew that the patient needed help and knew exactly what to do. After the patient was safe and taken care of, Fran was very thankful and realized that a doctor had helped her.

She thought he was very attractive with blue eyes and light brown hair. He had a chiseled face, which made him even more interesting to her. He was, of course, older than she was. He said, "If you were a little older, I would ask you out on a date."

Fran said, "I just suddenly aged five years." Dr. Mac was twenty-seven years old at that time, and Fran was barely eighteen years old. He said he liked the fact that she was bowlegged because his mother was bowlegged. It was definitely a mutual attraction.

He also had a very kind demeanor, which made her immediately feel at ease, even though he was a doctor, and she was "just" a radiology tech. Some of the doctors there liked to order everyone else around because they thought they were better.

They went out on several dates, even though her sisters felt like he was too old for her. After a while, they fell in love. She felt like he was her guardian angel, especially after all she had gone through with her mother. Her sisters grew to love him also when they realized how kind he was.

They had a small family wedding, and Mom (Fran) said she was so nervous on their honeymoon. She had blotted her lipstick on a piece of tissue and thrown it hurriedly into the commode. Mac made a comment about "the lips," and the rest was history. It is so refreshing to know that some people actually wait till after marriage to consummate the union.

Mac got a job at a very prestigious medical clinic in New Orleans. He was an internist and hematologist (concerned with blood diseases and what is now oncology). Fran stayed home and made friends with some of the other doctors' wives and played bridge and tennis. They didn't have much money, but they were happy.

Fran wanted to have a baby so badly. It took them seven years to finally have me. Apparently, Mac's sperm count was low, which caused the delay. Fran was twenty-six years old. I was born with strawberry blond hair and a personality to match it. Fourteen months later, my brother, Brad, was born. We were both born breech (buttocks or feet first) instead of the usual head first. It was usually a more difficult delivery, and to add to Fran's struggle, Brad was over ten pounds. That was a big baby. Mom said it nearly killed her. Everyone thought we were twins because Brad was so big, and I was so little. Brad had white hair, just like Mac had when he was born.

The Big Move Begins

FRAN HAD ALWAYS WANTED TO LIVE IN Florida where the weather was warm and the sandy white beaches beckoned all. Mac agreed and left his job at one medical clinic to find another job in a smaller medical clinic. He was one of three hematologists in the entire state of Florida at that time. The clinic was very happy to have him. He loved his job and his patients, and they loved him also.

We moved into a little middle-class neighborhood, where there were lots of kids for Brad and me to play with. I was three years old, and Brad was two. I made friends with five little girls who were all playing in the mud making mud pies. All the moms stayed home, and we played outside a lot and also had play days at one another's houses. We climbed trees, made forts, and swam in our neighbor's pool. Back then your kids could play outside without having to be concerned about their safety as much as you do now.

Dad quickly became the neighborhood doctor. We had a family of alcoholics on each side of us. I never had been around alcoholics and didn't understand the screaming and yelling on one side of us and the very quiet and withdrawn family on the other. I never saw my dad drink unless it was an occasional beer after going fishing. My parents went to parties, but I never once heard them argue about anything. The fact that Mac was very mellow made a huge difference, and Fran knew what a catch she had.

One night, Dad came rushing home and said he had just called 911 to come get one of the kids from next door at the quiet alcoholics' house. My dad went with little Ray, my neighbor, to the hospital. When he came back, he told us that Ray, who was about our age, had burned the entire torso of his body doing drugs. My dad said he almost died. I didn't know anything about drugs, and it scared me so badly that I swore never to do them.

Ray finally came home after a long hospital stay. He wouldn't take his shirt off to go swimming with us. He was embarrassed because of his burned body. I felt sorry for him, but it made a lasting impression on me. I never knew what kind of drug he did and always wondered why he did it. All I knew was that God had saved him for a reason. I heard years later that he had inherited a lot of money, but I was sure, if he had a chance to do it over again, he would rather have his healthy body back.

Dad also took care of another neighbor down the street who committed suicide by shooting her brains out. Her two-year-old son found her. Dad had to take care of all the arrangements. The young son always told my dad "thank you" for years afterward for being there to comfort him when it happened.

As I got a little older, Mom started playing tennis every day. We hired a black maid named Jossie. I adored her. She was always so cheerful and smiling. We used to talk about God a lot and how good He was to us.

One day, she started complaining of headaches. She never complained about anything. She was always singing gospel songs while she cleaned, and I could tell she was having a difficult time working. I told her I was going to talk to my dad about it.

That night, I told my dad about Jossie's headaches. He got her an appointment with one of our doctor friends who was a neurosurgeon. She was diagnosed with a brain tumor, and the doctor did the surgery for free because Jossie didn't have insurance.

That was an act of kindness, and Jossie was so thankful. She couldn't stop talking about it when she was back to normal. She kept saying that God had saved her for a reason, and I totally agreed with her. She cleaned the neurosurgeon's house for free after that.

It gave me a warm feeling in my heart about Dad's doctor friends at an early age, and I decided that I wanted to be a nurse when I was old enough so I could help people also. Little did I know that not all doctors were like my dad.

As I got a little older, I started getting interested in horses. Several of the neighborhood girls had horses, so my dad bought me a beautiful Tennessee Walker. He was jet-black with a smooth silky coat and long flowing mane and tail. His name was Midnight. He wouldn't let anyone ride him but me. I loved him so much. We kept him nearby at a friend's riding stable with lots of acreage.

My dad also bought me another very expensive horse, which we kept about two hours away. He was a gorgeous chestnut Arabian with a blonde mane and tail. His name was Galivar. My riding teacher had been part of a circus act with the horses. Her name was Dorita, and she was from Ukraine. She taught me how to ride dressage. It was a beautiful style of riding by using your hands, legs, and weight to guide the horse through a series of intricate movements. I felt very special to have Galivar and learn this new type of riding. My dad spoiled me so much, not only with things but also with love. Unfortunately, since Dorita lived two hours away, I usually ended up riding Midnight most of the time. I still loved Midnight, but Galivar was just such a novelty.

One day, while my friends and I were out riding bareback, Midnight suddenly pulled his head down. I was not prepared for him to do that, and I fell off him head first. The next thing I remember was waking up in the hospital with a horrible headache. I felt like I had a ton of weight on my head pushing me down to the floor when I stood up. I also was very light-headed and actually thought I was in heaven, but I didn't see any angels.

Apparently, I had been unconscious for the whole day, and my parents had just slipped downstairs to the cafeteria to get something to eat. When they came back, they were so happy to see me awake and immediately called for the doctor, who was a friend of my parents. My guardian angels were with me that day. I could have broken my neck or had brain damage. It was funny, but I was upset because the paramedics had to tear one of my favorite shirts off me.

They say you should always get right back up on your horse when you fell off no matter what. So when I was feeling better and able to ride again, Midnight and I continued to be best buddies. We eventually sold Galivar because of the drive, but I really loved and missed him also.

My parents joined the country club, and I started playing a lot of tennis and stupidly lying out in the sun by the pool with my friends. Most of them would get an easy tan, and I would sunburn because of my fair skin. If I knew what I know now, I would have worn more sunscreen and kept my sun time down to a minimum. A tan is so damaging to your skin, but living in Florida made it difficult not to want to be outside.

I didn't get to see my dad much because he worked such long hours, but my mom made sure we went to the beach for family vacations. Once my mom and I and my aunt were swimming in the ocean and got caught in an undertow. My mom kept trying to push me ahead of her, but I couldn't feel anything under my feet to stand on. The water kept pushing us further away from the shore. I was so frightened that we were going to die right there in the water. By a miracle, we got back on shore again. We were both exhausted. We looked for my aunt, and she was floating on her back a good distance out from shore. We called for the lifeguard, and he managed to get her back in by throwing her a big life tube on a long rope. It took several attempts, but thank God she was rescued. I really didn't want to go back to the beach for a good while after that.

Another way we got to spend time with our dad was to go hunting and fishing with him. We hunted quail and dove, and Mom made us some good meals with them. I caught a ten-pound bass when I was ten years old and was so proud of myself. We had it mounted.

Both my parents were animal lovers and we grew up always having animals. Of course, we had bird dogs; but we also had cats, fish, birds, and even a pet raccoon named Junior. I always thought there was something wrong with people who didn't like animals.

Mom took us to church every Sunday, and I actually sang in the choir with my friends. Dad was a deacon for a while, and he would take Brad and me with him to count the collection. It was fun to put the coins in the money rolls and to be with our dad. After church, we went out to the local buffet for lunch. People would come up to us and look down at me and tell me how wonderful my dad was, and I felt so proud to be his daughter. After lunch, he would go do hospital rounds and catch up on his charts.

I knew my mom felt like a single mom sometimes, but she knew he would always be home later and was a good provider, as well as a good man. I was sure women probably wanted my dad, but I would bet my life on it that he never cheated on her.

Teen Times

BY NOW, BRAD AND I WERE TEENAGERS. Boys were starting to become more important to me. Brad was very handsome with long blonde hair and blue eyes, and he got the skin that tanned easily. I was so envious of him for that. I also had long blonde hair and hazel eyes. We both were very fit and athletically built. He and his friends were really getting into surfing, and he would bring his surfing buddies over to play pool and just hang. With just fourteen months in our age difference, we were attracted to each other's friends, and they were attracted to us.

My first out-of-town encounter with boys was when I was fourteen years old, and our family went to Mexico City for vacation. We were at a museum, and two really cute Mexican boys kept following me around the museum and telling me how pretty I was. After we left, it made a lasting impression on me.

While we were in Mexico City, my dad mentioned to our tour guide that he had felt a slight tremor in the night. Our guide dismissed it as nothing, and the next day, we were in a full-blown earthquake. We were in our hotel room on the fourth floor, and we could feel the floor shaking and the building moving back and forth. Lamps were falling off the tables, and the chandelier fell off the ceiling. I could hear people screaming in the hotel, and all of a sudden, all the lights were out, and we had no electricity.

My mom shoved us all into a closet and started reciting the Lord's Prayer. I thought for sure we were going to die. Finally, after what seemed like hours, the floor stopped shaking, and we ventured out of the closet.

People were still screaming, but thank God everyone in our family was safe. Our hotel room was a mess, and when we went outside, there were huge cracks in the streets. The hotel was still standing, but it looked like a demolition crew had just come in.

No one was killed where we were, but in the city near us, several hundred people were dead. God had saved us, and we were so thankful. It made me sad, but we were ready to go home now.

Probably the most different thing we did besides being in an earthquake was go to the bullfights. I felt sorry for the bulls, but it was exciting to watch the matadors get so close to the bull and watch the clowns try to distract the bulls. All the spectators were yelling and screaming in Spanish with such enthusiasm that it was exhilarating.

Brad and my dad started getting interested in karate. Their style was called *shotokan*, which used a lot of kicking and punching. They both got their black belts and even went to Japan to study there. When they came back, their use of karate was considered a lethal weapon if they were ever in a fight besides in the dojo, a place where the martial arts were taught.

They brought back some of their instructors from Japan, and they were extremely amusing. They were all big with long black hair, and they always belched out loud burps after they ate. At first, I thought it was kind of rude but laughed anyway. Then I found out that it was their way of showing appreciation for my mom's dinner that she had made for them.

Brad was the quarterback at the private school he attended. Dad was the team doctor. I was a bit upset when Brad told me that one of the nuns was paying a little too much attention to him. He never told my parents, but I wanted to let the administration know about it. He told me not to get involved, and he would take care of it.

High school was like a party for me. My dad had bought me a nice Mustang for my first car, and I thought I was all that. I was part of the popular crowd, and we were pretty close. I didn't start drinking till my senior year, and we would usually end up in the orange groves just talking. We would also party at kids' houses whose parents weren't home. We especially liked going to the Hobsons' house. They owned multiple grocery stores and had a huge house. We never got caught, and thank God no one was ever hurt. I did throw up all over a friend's car from drinking too much, but we laugh about it now.

Pot was just getting popular around then, and some of the kids would get wasted out in the school parking lot. I was still afraid to do anything involving drugs because of what had happened to my neighbor burning himself when I was younger. Now I consider alcohol like a drug. I have seen too many alcoholics and too many DUIs. Also, as a nurse, I have seen ascites, the accumulation of fluid in the peritoneal cavity, which causes abdominal swelling. It makes a person look like they are pregnant and also causes jaundice, a medical condition with yellowing of the skin and eyes due to liver damage. Yet alcohol is legal and pot isn't.

I had several boyfriends but never wanted to stay with just one. I thought it was more fun to be with different guys and do different things that they were interested in. I watched some of my girlfriends stay with one guy through high school and all the drama they went through. I didn't want to have anything to do with it.

I was rather concerned, though, when some of my father's doctor friends hit on me. I had to have a skin exam by one of the dermatologists at the clinic, and he knew my parents. It was rather embarrassing because I had to take off all my clothes, and he looked at every inch of my body. He even looked at my vaginal area, which I really didn't expect, nor did I think it was absolutely necessary. He said that melanomas could be anywhere on your body, which was true.

He came to one of my parents' cocktail parties at our house. My mom always wanted me to be the cocktail waitress at her parties. I did it mainly for her, but I enjoyed talking to her friends also. Well, Dr. Dickhead, the dermatologist who had done my skin exam, told me how nice my body was when I handed him his drink. Not only was it unprofessional but his timing was very poor. I just wanted to leave the house.

Another time, our family went on a trip to the Bahamas. My friends in high school used to call me Bahama Mama. We went with another one of my dad's friends who was a surgeon. He was very nice-looking with thick wavy black hair, big brown eyes, and a great smile. He also was a huge flirt. He had married his high school sweetheart, and I wondered why she put up with him.

Several years after that vacation, I worked at the clinic he and my dad worked at. He came into the office room that I was working in and started flirting with me. I found it amusing at first, until he asked me to go out of town on a dinner date with him. He was twice my age, and it would have been too weird for me. He had recently divorced. I found it interesting that he later married a woman who was a little blonde like me. His first wife had black hair and was so sweet. They were both Cajuns.

We went on another cruise to the Bahamas with just our family. By then, Mom and Dad let us have more freedom since we were older. I met some kids there about my age, and we had fun together. One night, on my way to my room, one of the officers on the ship asked me for a drink. I was underage, and I told him so, and then he asked me if I would like a tour of the ship. He was a very nice-looking young man, older by at least five or six years. He showed me places on the ship that the average guest would not be able to see. When we were finished with the tour, we ended up in his room. I was rather intimidated and naive and didn't realize he was trying to seduce me. He was practically trying to rape me. I told him to get off me and started screaming. I was sure it was against the ship's policy to fraternize with the guests, especially underage. He finally got off me, and I ran out the door. I was so upset, but I didn't want to talk about it to anyone that night. I ended up telling my dad what happened after the trip, and of course, he was very upset and angry. God saved me again.

I was snorkeling the next day out by the reefs to look at all the pretty fish and coral when, all of a sudden, I looked up, and a boatload of natives was yelling at me to get out of the water. Apparently, I was swimming in a school of barracudas. I hadn't even noticed. My guardian angels were all over me again. I lost my desire to go back to the Bahamas any time soon.

The Vietnam War broke out when I was a sophomore in high school. The draft was horrible then and unfair. Many of the kids were trying to get out of being drafted by moving to Canada or claim that they had some illness. Back then claiming to be gay was an issue considered not favorable to being recruited. Even now, the thought of making an eighteen-year-old fight in a war upsets me. I was so glad my brother wasn't old enough.

I had several friends who were ahead of me in high school who were drafted, and they all came back wanting to get married. It was very traumatic for them and a sad time for many mothers and families when they heard their sons were killed in action or missing in action.

The Vietnam veterans never really got the recognition they deserved or the help they needed. It was all just a senseless mistake. Most of the guys came back with some type of post-traumatic stress syndrome and never got treatment for it.

Graduation and College-Bound

I FINALLY GRADUATED FROM HIGH SCHOOL, AND I was still a virgin. Back then if you got pregnant, you went out of town to have your baby, but everybody knew anyway. I had a good GPA, and my SAT scores were good, so I had several options of colleges I could go to. My mom took me on a tour to look at some rich-bitch girls' schools, but I ended up going to the local state university.

The main reason was because I had worked as a lifeguard that summer with a gorgeous football player from my high school. He was two years older than I was and asked me up for the weekend. I stayed with one of our cheerleader friends from high school and went to his fraternity party. I thought I was all that not just being with him but also being at a fraternity party at seventeen years old. The only reason my mom let me go was because she knew his parents from church. He talked me into going to the University locally.

Another one of my high school girl friends talked me into rooming with her in the school dorms. It was the first year they had co-ed dorms, so it was a big deal. The guys were on one floor, and the girls were on the other. It was the era of "burn the bra" with a group of lesbians marching past the picket lines.

It started out okay, but my friend's boyfriend was always there, and he even had to pee in a bottle in our room one night because he was there after hours. It was kind of noisy, but it was a great way to meet other people.

Wow! It was a huge university for me at seventeen years old. With no parents to be accountable for, the freshmen were all going wild with their new freedom. The boys were everywhere, and I wasn't prepared for all the attention I was getting, but I liked it.

On my first day there, I was walking through the tennis court area when I heard someone yell at me from across, "Hey, Blondie!" A tall blond, blue-eyed guy came running up to me. He was very forward, I thought, since I had just met him. I was sure he assumed I was a freshman since the tennis courts were right in front of the freshman dorm. He asked me out on the spot, and I was kind of scared. Since I didn't know anything about him, I agreed to meet him at a local diner near campus later.

We got together, and he told me his name was Bo. He was a graduate student in journalism. He was twenty-two years old, which was a little intimidating to me, but I was curious about him, and he was a good tennis player with a nice smile. I agreed to go out with him the next night. He picked me up in his nice sports car, a GTO, and we ended up at a strip club. I had never been to a strip club before, and when I saw those half-naked women dancing around the poles, I felt completely out of place. I was sure Bo was amused by my reaction.

I was not sure how I got to stay there because it was obvious that I was underage. Everyone there knew Bo, so I assumed that was why the owner didn't say anything. I was so uncomfortable there, though, that I was soon ready to leave.

Bo lived in a nice apartment with a gorgeous roommate. I really wanted to be with him, but he was with another girl. He was from California, and it was obvious that he wasn't lacking in the money department.

I decided to go through the sorority game but decided it was too superficial for me. Some of the girls seemed really nice, but some of them were so snobby that it made me sick. I decided to drop out.

Then one night, while I was taking a shower in the dorm's shower room, I heard some girls' voices calling my name. I opened the shower curtain barely, and they were two girls I had met from one of the nicer, well-known sororities. They asked me to reconsider pledging to their sorority. They were so sweet and genuine about it, so I ended up pledging. I was glad I did because I met some really nice girls there.

Bo and I continued to see each other for a while even though I went out with other guys I met mostly around the dorm. The fact that Bo was older and had a car made him more appealing to me at that time.

Well, to make a long story short, I ended up losing my virginity to him. I was extremely disappointed. After all I had heard about having an orgasm and how great it was, it was a big letdown. Even though I knew I shouldn't have done it, I guess I was glad I finally found out what it was all about. I did feel guilty, though. At that time, I wasn't as close to God as I am now, plus I was "young and dumb." God's grace saved me from getting pregnant. I lost interest in Bo after that, even though he still wanted to be with me.

There was a guy who lived in the dorm on the other side of the tennis courts. He was also nice-looking with long dark hair. We used to walk to our first class together every morning after he smoked a joint very discreetly. Back in the '70s, a lot of people smoked pot, but I was still afraid to. Lou was extremely smart and a surfer. I really liked him, and we had a lot of fun together.

He had a roommate who had a pet boa constrictor, which I wasn't real fond of at first. I eventually got used to him. Lou's roommate, Jack, was interested in being a veterinarian and finally got in later. It was difficult to get in because there were less vet schools than there were med schools.

I stopped dating Lou, even though I really liked him. When I found out that he was a virgin, in a strange way, I felt like I would be corrupting him. He and his roommate were really hurt by it, but I just felt it was for the best. I heard later that he had become a cardiac surgeon. I guess smoking all that pot didn't ruin his motivation at all.

Two of my guy friends were already at the university before me. Chad had become somewhat of a hippie type. In high school, he had been a popular preppie type on the school golf team. His father was a pro. I always had a crush on him in high school. Now he had long dark hair down to his shoulders and a very contagious smile. We were good friends, and he never pushed me into having sex with him. We would go to concerts and weekend music festivals together. Sometimes people would walk around naked, but we weren't into that.

I went to pot parties with him for about a year before I asked him if I could try it. He said, "Are you sure?"

I said, "Yes, because you are the only person I trust doing it with." So he showed me how to roll a joint and how to suck in and blow out through either my mouth or my nose. Of course, I gagged and coughed and wondered what it was all about, and then it hit me.

Everything was so slow, and Chad was so sweet. We sat around, talked for hours, then got really hungry, and stuffed ourselves at the closest twenty-four-hour fast-food drive-through. We went back to his place and fell asleep. I woke up the next morning with my best friend next to me. I felt like my first encounter with marijuana had been a success.

Phil was another high school friend whom I hung around. He was in the same fraternity that Chad was in. Phil was more athletic in a different way. He was tall and muscular and had long honey-colored hair. We went fishing a lot and just had fun being together. He did magic mushrooms, though, and I really was afraid to do that. He tried to talk me into trying it, but I said no.

Phil was very much into skydiving. He was one of the guys who did the star formations with other skydivers. Phil asked me one night while we were at his fraternity house at a party if I would want to try skydiving. It looked like it would be a lot of fun, so I said yes. I called my parents and told them what I was planning on doing, and my dad was very concerned, of course. He made me promise to call them after I had jumped.

The next day, Phil took me out to the skydiving school and introduced me to the instructors. I was really nervous but had decided I was going to do it. After we had our instructional class, they helped me with my gear and helmet and put the parachute on me. We all got into the plane, and we had already discussed the fact that the instructor on the plane would pull the cord for my parachute automatically from the plane. When we got high enough to jump, I jumped out of the plane saying a prayer. They pulled the cord, and I felt like I was floating in heaven. It was extremely quiet, and there were white clouds all around me. It was such a cool experience, and they even got a picture of me before I landed.

I jumped a second time doing the same static line technique that I did the first time. They pulled the cord for me again, but this time, I landed too much on my feet and didn't roll enough. I sprained my ankle and had to stop jumping. I had my ankle wrapped and had to have my friends push me all over campus in a wheelchair. I think my parents were relieved that I didn't want to jump again.

Phil ended up marrying a beautiful girl who got in a car accident, and it scarred her whole face. I heard she didn't want to stay married to him because she felt so ugly and didn't want him to feel like he had to stay with her. He loved her, though, and wanted to stay married. I don't know if they made it or not. I don't know who I felt worse for. This world would be so much better if we could just love ourselves and others for our inside beauty. If we all looked alike, then we would fall in love with the person's heart first. Often, an attractive person is taken advantage of or becomes narcissistic.

There was another guy, Charles, who was also in the same fraternity as Chad and Phil. He was a little older, a senior in the engineering field. He was the nicest guy and such a gentleman. He told Chad and Phil he was interested in being with me, so we went to dinner and dated awhile. He liked his scotch, but he didn't do drugs. I called him my movie star because he had such an air of sophistication and class. Looking back, he was one of the guys I should have stayed with.

I decided it was time to meet some guys from a different fraternity and went to a party with some of my sorority sisters. I met Skyler there. He had the prettiest thick curly blond hair I had ever seen and big brown eyes. He was so sweet and kept telling me all the time how much he loved me. We went to the beach together during beach week, and he told me he wanted to marry me. I couldn't handle that. I told him it would have to be in the far future.

I was such a diva. I got mad at him at one of the fraternity parties, dumped my beer all over his head right in front of everyone, and then walked away. He ended up living on a houseboat, and last I heard, he is happily married to a girl he met at the university. I am happy for him because he deserved someone who would appreciate him.

I started jogging around the track at the university. It was good exercise and a good way to meet people. I even participated in a running experiment that some engineering students were doing as a school project. We were supposed to run and keep up with a lighting system as we ran around the track.

As I was running one very hot day during the experiment, I suddenly went totally blind. I was freaking out, not knowing what was going on. Thank God there was a coach there who told me I was experiencing heat exhaustion. He held my hand and put me under a tree for shade and gave me some salt tablets and water. I finally got my vision back and was so thankful that the coach and God helped me. It was so scary. I decided not to participate in the experiment anymore.

I decided I would just jog around the campus because there were so many jogging trails everywhere. One evening around dusk, I was jogging on one of the trails in front of the fraternity houses that had a small section of trees and bushes surrounding it. There was a guy standing in the middle of the path, and I thought he was waiting for me so we could jog together. It was common to pick up running partners on campus.

By the time I had run by him, expecting him to just follow along beside me, he grabbed me and threw me on the ground. We were still surrounded by the trees and bushes, so no one could see us. He started ripping my clothes off me and then got on top of me. I started screaming and tried to get him off me, but he was too heavy. Then I said, "Jesus, help me." He immediately got off me and started running away. I was in shock. I didn't know what to do next but thank my guardian angels for saving me again.

I wasn't going to tell anybody but ended up confiding with the first young couple I saw. They said they had a friend at the campus police department, and they took me there. I couldn't believe that the cop actually asked me if it really happened. I asked him why he would think I would make up something like that. My clothes were dirty and torn. It was very obvious and embarrassing.

He said that women lied all the time about it just to get attention. I told him I got more than enough attention and that it definitely happened. He asked if I would testify, but I said no because I didn't get a good look at his face. He just looked like any other student on campus with no distinguishing features. He had dark hair and jogging clothes on. After that incident, I always ran with a friend.

I was beginning to get a little bored at the university. I wasn't sure what I wanted to do since my dad still didn't want me to be a nurse. I was tired of the fraternity/sorority scene and wanted to do something different.

My mom and dad were both athletic and liked to travel. Our family went to Aspen, Colorado, to go snow skiing for the Christmas holidays. We knew absolutely nothing about snow skiing, so we took lessons from a very nice-looking instructor from Austria. He had a lot of patience with us, especially with my parents. Soon we were skiing on our own.

It was so beautiful there with the big "Christmas trees" everywhere covered with snow. The hotel was fabulous, and we had fun in the

Jacuzzi and sauna. Brad and I met a lot of teenagers there who went to the university nearby. They kept encouraging me to transfer there.

I thought about it more when we got home because we had so much fun out there. I had bought a poster while I was in Colorado. It was a picture of two guys on a ski lift smoking a joint, and it said, "Ski Stoned." I put it up on my wall above the head of my bed in the dorm to inspire me to study harder.

I had partied a lot during my first semester, and my grades were not that good. I was determined to make good grades this next semester to get my grade point average up. Thank God my trigonometry teacher liked me. He literally gave me a five-hour A. I was so thankful for his generosity, but he said I deserved it because I went in every day for help. I didn't understand trigonometry, so I needed the help. I think he liked my short shorts too.

I studied really hard and cut way down on the partying. I got my grade point average up, mailed out my transcripts to the university in Colorado, and prayed I would get in. The miracle happened, and I was accepted. I was so excited.

Rocky Mountain Adventures

I WAS NINETEEN YEARS OLD AND ON my way to a new adventure. I didn't know a single person in Colorado except some of the kids I had met skiing. I thanked my parents for giving me this opportunity. I would miss my family, but there were always vacations.

My mom bought me a really nice outfit to wear on the plane. I even got a professional picture made in it. It meant a lot to me for my mom to actually buy me clothes because most of my clothes in high school were made by my aunt. She was an excellent seamstress, but I just wanted to have a few store-bought clothes. My mom had just wanted to keep my aunt busy because she started drinking when her husband died.

I will never forget getting on the bus that took me to the University. It was absolutely breathtaking! As we got closer and closer to the mountains, I got more and more excited. There was another guy on the bus who said he was a student at the University. He was rather rugged looking with long hair and a beard. He told me about the special mountains there that all the students had to climb to be considered "cool". Thankfully, I met a cute guy there who just happened to be a professional mountain climber. He took me up to the top of the mountain using ropes and pitons like the real professionals do. It was very scary, and he told me not to look down, so I just hung on for fear of falling. I was so happy when we finally got to the top. We decided to just hike down and take our time, but I was glad I actually did it.

I decided to live in the dorm since I really didn't know anyone, and I thought it would be a good way to meet other people. My roommate was from Denver. She was very sweet but not very attractive and a little overweight. We immediately liked each other, though, and we got to be good friends. She told me about her boyfriend and how cool she had thought he was in high school. He had been a star basketball player, and she didn't think she would ever get be with him. When I met him, I thought he was nice but not someone I would be interested in, thank God. I was happy for Carla, my roommate, because she was so in love.

Living in the dorm out west was very different from living at the dorm back home. The guys were allowed there anytime. I was the only one from Florida, and a lot of the kids joked around with me about my southern accent. I kind of stuck out like a sore thumb also because I dressed differently than they did. I wore makeup and nice clothes, and most of them didn't wear makeup and wore jeans and T-shirts. Where we lived before we came to school was on a poster on the front of our dorm room doors. Everybody wanted to meet me because they knew I was coming from Florida. It made meeting people even more fun for me.

I met a girl who was in the pre nursing program, and I was very envious. Deep down inside, I really still wanted to be a nurse. I also met a hippie-type girl from the East, whom I ended up giving a Bible to. She thanked me later for helping her become a Christian, and I felt so blessed to be able to help her.

The campus was absolutely gorgeous with the mountains always visible and the huge fir trees. My first Fall there was fabulous with the beautiful leaves all changing into bright yellows, oranges, and reds. I actually got down on the ground in the middle of the leaves and made leaf angels like a child. My friends thought it was funny, but I was in heaven.

The longer I was there, the more I became like a hippie Colorado kid. I traded in my bright red pants and bought a secondhand pair of worn old jeans. A lot of the styles now were popular in the seventies. We wore long flowing skirts and big embroidered tops. I still wore my Florida short shorts, though, when the weather permitted. I didn't want to give them up.

I decided to continue my major in recreational therapy for the handicapped. I still wanted to do something where I could help people. My classes were varied. Some were difficult, and some were easy. Molecular cellular developmental biology was the most difficult for me, like trigonometry had been. I didn't know why I had to take it, but it was a required class for my major. I got blessed again, and the teacher's assistant liked me and helped tutor me.

He had a motorcycle, and we would cruise through the winding mountain roads. It was so much fun. I knew it was dangerous, but at that time, I didn't care. Finn was just a nice friend and never pushed our relationship further. Instead of getting a D, I ended up passing with a C. I was very grateful for this and thanked Finn for helping me.

My roommate, Carla, was a Pentecost. She invited me to her Pentecostal church. I had been raised Presbyterian and was kind of freaked out at first when I heard everyone speaking in tongues and laying on of hands. I had not ever heard anyone prophesize. Everyone was so nice, and it was cool to have a church service in the mountains. I felt like I was in God's country, peaceful and natural.

I continued to go to the church and met a lady, Marin, who owned a Christian bookstore. She had a defective eye that drooped and gave her a sad appearance, but she was a very positive woman and never complained about it. We became friends, and she asked me if I would like to fill in at times and work at her bookstore. I said yes and got exposed to some really good Christian books and met some very nice people while working there.

I liked Marin and felt a little sorry for her because of her drooping eye. She started asking me for money to help pay for her medical bills. I didn't mind at first, but then I felt like she was taking advantage of me. I didn't want to feel guilty for saying no, yet it was getting to be more and more often. I thought it best for us to just go our separate ways rather than end up with resentment.

I thanked Carla for introducing me to her church and told her how I wished I could be more like she was. She told me that she and her boyfriend were sleeping together, and even though they both knew it was wrong, they were still doing it. I was glad that she felt comfortable enough to tell me that. I felt like she was telling me that because, even though she was a Christian, she wasn't perfect and was sinning. I told her I understood what she was saying and that I would pray for her that it worked out for them to stay together.

I decided to check out the fraternity scene, even though I had been told it wasn't cool there. I had met a few frat boys, but they weren't as much fun as the others. I went to a fraternity party because a famous band was there. The drummer of the band came up to me after the party was over and asked me to go to his hotel room with the rest of the band for a small party there. I said yes only because there would be other people there, and after all, he was the drummer in a cool band.

Rugby was a popular sport there. I got to know some of the rugby players, and some of my girl friends and I became rugger huggers. Rugger huggers were like cheerleaders, only better. One of the players had two Great Danes, which took up practically the whole van. Another lived with one of my girl friends, and she cooked and cleaned for him even though he was cheating on her. She was a beautiful girl, and my girl friends and I kept telling her to leave him, but for some stupid reason, she stayed.

I got tired of living in the dorm and ended up living in an old house with beautiful aspen trees in the yard. My roommates were three other girls and a guy. We each had our own rooms, and mine was huge with a big picture window. I loved living there.

The first day I moved in, the girls were eating lunch at the kitchen table. We hadn't met one another yet because I had answered an ad in the newspaper. One of the girls, who was really skinny, kept talking about how red the tomatoes were. I thought, *What a weirdo*, and she really was. I didn't know at that time that she was tripping on LSD right there in front of me. It kind of scared me, but I knew we wouldn't be hanging out together.

The other two girls were Carrie and Kelly. Carrie was about twenty-five years old and taught handicapped people how to snow ski. She taught people without an arm or without a leg and even blind people. I admired her for what she did. She came home crying one night and said she had a crush on one of the guys she worked with, but he liked the pretty girl who wore all the makeup. Carrie had beautiful, thick wavy brown hair and beautiful skin, but she was a little overweight.

Well, we had a makeover session, and I put some makeup on her and fixed her hair. She watched everything I did, and the next day, she went to work looking like a different woman. She grinned from ear to ear when she saw herself in the mirror. She came home that day and said he paid more attention to her, and she felt like she had more of a chance with him now. I was happy for her.

Kelly was closer to my age, nineteen years old. She was an athletic-looking tall type with thick long brown hair down to her waist and big brown eyes. She was really pretty, especially when she smiled. She was the typical student who always wore jeans and no makeup. We didn't get along at first, but by the end of my stay there, we were good friends. I became more of a hippie type, and she dressed up more and occasionally wore makeup. We smoked pot together every once in a while.

The guy, Dan, lived in the basement. He was very quiet, and I could tell he was already henpecked by the other girls. I felt sorry for him and tried to be nice to him.

The girls and I would go out occasionally together but didn't become close friends. I was so different from them. Also, they were all from the East, and I was definitely southern. We did go out to dinner one night to a very exclusive restaurant to celebrate Carrie's birthday. It was nestled up in the mountains, and the food was delicious; so was our waiter, Hunter. He had dark hair, blue eyes, and a very charming smile and demeanor.

While he was waiting on our table, it was obvious that he was flirting with me. He was from Georgia, and it was nice to talk to another southerner. The other girls noticed and started making comments about it to me. They were really jealous when he asked me out, but I wasn't about to say no because of them.

He picked me up in his bright orange BMW, which I thought was a bit weird. After dinner, we went to his house, and I met his roommate and his dog. He loved my Mercedes and said he had always wanted one. We dated for a while, but he had to go back to Georgia to have thyroid surgery. I saw him several years later in Aspen with one girl on each arm. I immediately recognized him, but I stepped out of his view. He was just too narcissistic for me.

I went to Denver to a disco place with a nice guy I met on campus. It was so much fun. The dance floor lit up in different colors to the rhythm of the music. That was the time of strobe lights and high energy on the dance floor. We also went camping in the mountains in a tent. It started getting really cold, and he told me if we got naked that our body heat would keep each other warm. I knew he was right, but I didn't feel like getting anything started with him, so I froze.

I met my first expert snow skier. He was on the university ski team. His name was Jacque, and he was very funny and attractive. We went to a restaurant, and he said he noticed that two guys kept looking at me. I told him not to worry about it, that I was with him. He went over to talk to them anyway and ended up in a fistfight. I was so embarrassed, and of course, they kicked us out. I had to clean up his face.

Life was getting a little too tense in the big house, so I decided it was time for me to move out before things got worse. I would miss Kelly but not the others. We said our good-byes.

I found a place to live with three other girls closer to campus. The area was called "the Hill." It was smaller, and I shared a room, but I had more in common with these girls. We got along much better.

My roommate was named Una. She was part Norwegian. She had black curly hair, blue eyes, and beautiful skin. She was overweight but still very pretty and very smart. Her parents were divorced, but she got to visit both of them, who lived in a city nearby. Her mother was a teacher and spoke three languages, and her father was an engineer and very controlling.

Una was a hard worker and studier. I would be coming home at 2:00 a.m. from partying, and she would be coming home from working at the doughnut shop and start studying. She was so motivated, and I really admired her.

Una struggled with her weight, though. She was always telling me I needed to eat more. She reminded me of my mother sometimes. By now, I was a vegan. I carried a bag of sunflower seeds around my waist. I was already thin and lost twelve pounds since high school. I really didn't need to lose any more and was becoming somewhat anorexic.

Una became influenced by my anorexic tendencies. One day, after she had taken a shower, she sat down in front of me with no shirt on. I was shocked when I saw her. She looked like a skeleton. I could easily see every rib on her torso. It made me sick to look at her. I told her she was way too skinny and I was concerned about her. She always was an extremist.

She ended up in the hospital and gradually started gaining her weight back. We decided to drive back to Florida together. I wanted her to meet my family, and she had never been to Florida before. She drove me crazy trying to stuff food in my face the whole way there. I tried to tell her I had always been small boned and thin. I took after my dad, who was a two-pound twin.

When I took her to the beach, she was just like a little kid, the way I had been when I saw my first Fall in Colorado. It was fun to watch her so happy making sand castles and splashing in the ocean waves. She had been working so hard and studying long hours that she definitely deserved a break.

Una ended up being a pediatric pathologist. I wasn't surprised. She was so motivated and determined. I haven't seen her for years, but I have fond memories of her. I will always remember her telling me that no matter what anybody said about me or to me, I should always hold my head high. Women can be so vicious to each other. God has helped me hold my head high to this day.

I moved again to another apartment, which was further from campus, but I had my own room. There were prairie dogs living in a field next to us. It was fun to watch them scurry to and from their little holes they had dug to live in.

One of my roommates was Lydia. She was a pretty tall brunette from Wisconsin. I loved to listen to her talk. Audra was from Durango, and she was a fun person to be with. She had wild curly blond hair and a deep, raspy voice. Tarah was a diva from Carmel, California. We were all four different from one another, but we got along well, accepting one another's idiosyncrasies.

We lived at the bottom of a hill, and I liked riding my bike to campus. One night, I was riding home, and I hit a rock in the road going downhill. My bike started tipping forward, and I knew I was going to crash. I lost control of my bike and started praying for God's help. I was going so fast that there was no way I could gain control of my bike again. All of a sudden, my bike totally leveled out and I was able to take control. It was as if my guardian angels were in full control of my bike. I had no more difficulties the rest of the way home. God saved me again.

Audra had an uncle and aunt who were very wealthy, and they invited us to dinner at their house in Denver. Her uncle was a big-time attorney. While we were having cocktails before dinner, Audra's uncle kept flirting with me and asked me if I would be interested in going out with him. Yes, he was very handsome, wealthy, and sophisticated; but he was married. I said no.

He then proceeded to hit on Tarah. Tarah said yes and started seeing him. We all told her not to do it, especially Audra, since it was her aunt that he was cheating on. It caused a lot of stress for Audra and Tarah. I felt like Tarah had a low self-esteem but couldn't understand how she could do that to Audra.

Audra wanted to get away from Tarah for the weekend, so we drove my little Mercedes through the mountains for our get-away. Being from

Florida, I wasn't familiar with mountain driving, and I didn't realize that I was driving too fast. Audra didn't say anything to me. I ended up skidding to the side of the road, and a policeman stopped me. He noticed my Florida license plate, and I told him I didn't realize I was going too fast. He was a nice cop and just gave me a ticket for improper mountain driving instead of reckless driving. I was so thankful.

I also hitchhiked around town when I didn't feel like riding my bike or trying to find a parking place, which was next to impossible. Looking back, I could have really gotten myself into trouble but never had a close call. I got picked up by a garbage truck and rode on top of the truck with the other guys. It was rather amusing to be sitting there with a pile of trash in front of me. I ended up giving one of the guys a Bible I had with me. He seemed very appreciative. Another time, I got picked up by two very nicely dressed black men. They were in a small sports car, so I had to squish into the back of the car. I think they were gay by the way they were talking to each other and to me. I started thinking that I could have been stuck in that car, and nobody would even know I was in there. They dropped me off at school, and I wiggled out of the car. They thought it was funny. They were very nice.

I was starting to get a little homesick now and decided to go to the social center on campus. They were showing a ski movie, and I thought watching it might get me motivated enough to want to stay in school there. I sat down in an empty seat on the end of the row in the back of the theater just before the movie started. Soon after I sat down, a guy with thick long strawberry blonde hair and a mustache sat down next to me and started talking to me.

There was something about him that intrigued me. He had a different accent that I couldn't figure out. He told me he was from Canada, and he was responsible for showing the movie. It was mainly about ski jumping, which I knew nothing about except water ski jumping. The movie was awesome. Sal, the guy who sat next to me, told me he was the captain of the ski jumping team at the University. I didn't know whether to believe him or not or if he was just trying to impress me.

After the movie was over, he invited me out for a drink. Back then I was so used to being asked out by guys whom I didn't know very well that I said yes. I also knew that he was indeed responsible for showing the movie because, after it was finished, he had to go talk to the rest of the crew.

We went to a quaint little bar and sat and drank and laughed for several hours. Of course, he made fun of the way I talked, and I made fun of the way he talked. He was so funny and very easy to talk to. He was sophisticated in a down-to-earth way.

He told me his father owned a big lumber company in Canada, and the only way to get there was by plane or helicopter. I was very impressed. It was obvious that he was a spoiled brat, but at least he was getting a business degree at the university. He was three years older than I was, and I loved how he wined and dined me and made me laugh.

He took me up into the mountains to his house. I was so impressed that he actually lived in the mountains. It was not a huge house, but it was all windows, and you could see the mountains all around. I loved it, and I really liked Sal a lot.

He had a roommate, who was hardly ever there because he was a famous professional skier. I never had a chance to meet him. He was murdered by the wife of a movie star. Sal's roommate and she had been having an affair, and she got jealous when she saw him with someone else. Her husband got her off somehow with his fancy, money-hungry lawyers. Sal was very distraught over the situation, and it made me very sad to see a young life wasted over cheating.

I ended up practically living with Sal. I would spend so much time in the mountains and would even do my homework there. One day, I was sitting up on a small cliff near the house where I had made a little space to read. I was reading a Christian book about deer and how they were able to climb the mountains by carefully putting one hoof in front of the other. The book was comparing the deer climbing the mountains to how we, as human beings, need to climb our "mountains" and experience valleys by carefully putting our faith in Jesus, knowing that each step we take would put us where He wanted us to be, as long as we trust Him to show us. Anyway, I looked up, and there was a deer just a few feet away from me. I was almost able to touch it. I felt like God had sent the deer to me as a sign of His forever presence on my journey through life. I told Sal about it, but he didn't really feel the same way I did about God. He believed, but I thought about Him more.

Sal and I went skiing together for the first time. I would never forget the first time I saw him ski jump right in front of me. It was so awesome how he flew through the air and kept right on going. His whole body was straight as an arrow pointed forward, with his ski tips hanging from his feet. It was such a special time for me to see that. He landed perfectly on the snow. I started clapping and screaming like a little kid. He liked me being so excited about his performance.

We decided to go to Aspen for the weekend with some of our friends, and he asked me to bring some pot along. I had never bought any myself, so I wasn't sure who to go to. I ended up asking one of the Hispanic guys who worked at the dorm cafeteria to help me out. He had always been extra nice to me, and I could tell that he liked me.

I made arrangements to meet him at his house and pick it up. When I got there, he said we needed to "test it out" together. I thought, *Okay, it can't hurt just to try it.* It was very potent pot, and we ended up getting super stoned. Sal didn't know where I was. He was upset with me when I finally got home, especially when he found out that I smoked with the guy I got it from. It was all perfectly innocent on my part. We didn't do anything even though he wanted to. Sal got over it when he saw my big smile when I pulled out the full bag of pot. I felt kind of guilty about it but was glad I could get it for all of us for the weekend. We got stoned the whole way to Aspen in Sal's big red van. We decided to take it since it was bigger, and we had two other skiers from the team with us and their girlfriends. The music was blaring so loud that I was sure they could hear us coming.

We had a blast in Aspen. The snow conditions were perfect. Sal had bought me my first pair of really nice skis from a ski shop that was owned by several of his French friends. They were excellent skiers also. Sal took me to the top of the expert run, and I was so angry with him. He was an expert skier, and I was a beginner. The run had huge moguls everywhere, and it took me practically all day to get down the mountain. I will have to give Sal credit, though, because he was very patient with me. He actually thought it was funny, and after a while, I started getting better, and it became more fun. He was a good teacher, and I knew I was safe with him.

The nightlife in Aspen was fantastic. There were several movie stars there, and it was fun to see them. There were a variety of restaurants and bars to choose from. The night's crisp air was so exhilarating, and the night lights were beautiful. Sal went up to the bar to get us some drinks, and this random guy came up to me and told me he had been watching me all night at the bar. He quickly asked me for my phone number, and I gave it to him, thinking I would probably never see him again. I was half drunk already. I was never a good drinker. It always made me sleepy and horny. It was good to get home safely.

Sal was constantly amusing me. When we were at his house, he used to like to put on his robe and pretend like he was a male stripper. He cracked me up. I never saw him down. He was always happy, and his friends told me they had never seen him spend so much time with one girl except me. We just got along so well.

I had the feeling that Sal thought we were going to get married, but I knew I was way too young. I took him with me to visit my family when they came out to ski from Florida. For some reason, my mother told me later that she didn't think he was the best choice for me. She didn't explain why, though, and I have always wondered what her reason was. I knew she overdramatized that we were a very southern family. I made a decision then to break off our relationship and told him as we were sitting on the ski lift that I wanted to remain friends and how much I valued his friendship.

I moved on, and all his friends said I broke his heart. I felt really bad about it, but I knew myself well enough to know that I wasn't mature enough for a permanent relationship yet. Maybe I should have married him. I didn't know. It would have been a much different life than the one I had later, but thank God, He is always with us.

Apparently, Sal went a little crazier than usual and started drinking too much after we broke up. He was found on the side of the mountain wrecked in his once-beautiful Porsche after being there several hours in the melting snow. It was a miracle that he lived through it. He ended up getting a steel plate in his head, which was so typical of him. I felt really bad for him, though.

By now, I had met a lot of people and had a lot of fun. I had finished three years of college and had an opportunity to do an early internship in England. My parents said yes, and I was so excited. There was one other girl from the Department of Recreational Therapy for the Handicapped going also. Her name was Lisa. At least I would know one person there.

Internship and Europe

MY MAJOR IN ENGLAND WAS CALLED REMEDIAL gymnastics. I really wanted to help people and thought this was something I would like doing. Lisa felt the same way I did, and we became friends while we were in school together.

I told my family good-bye and thanked my parents again for giving me this opportunity. I was thankful that my mom liked to travel so much and that we could afford it. The flight to England was very long. We watched movies, read magazines, and listened to music. I had to take some over-the-counter anti nausea medicine so I wouldn't get motion sickness.

We finally arrived and were picked up by one of the students there in the school van. It was amusing to listen to him talk with his strong English accent. He told us how excited the other students were to meet us. We were the only ones from the United States. He dropped us off at a hospital that was temporarily used as a dorm for fourteen other girls. We stayed there for about a month. The other girls and guys were from England, Wales, Scotland, and Ireland. One of the girls, Marni, was from Canada. She was very independent and had already traveled the world.

The second month, I moved into an apartment—which they called a flat—with two English girls, Tiff and Melli. They had two cats, and we had so much fun together. We lived in the country part of England called Yorkshire. I loved the outdoor markets, the pastry shops, the little fish-and-chips takeout down the street, and the Yorkshire pudding.

The countryside was just beautiful there. We went horseback riding, and they gave me the most spirited stallion they had. I told them I had

ridden a lot in my younger years. He was really fast, and it was so much
fun to ride down the country roads. The people there were extremely
friendly, and the girls and I hitchhiked all over Ossett, the little town
we lived in.

One of my roommates, Tiff, had a boyfriend who lived in Liverpool,
where the Beatles were from. He would come and visit on the weekends.
Even though we were both speaking English, we couldn't understand
each other. He had a very thick English accent, and I had a southern
drawl, so it was rather comical when we tried to talk to each other.
Finally, by the end of my stay, we could actually understand each other.

I went to a party and met a guy who had a very wealthy father. He
drove a nice Jaguar and seemed like a nice guy but was rather quiet. Pub
hopping was the main entertainment over there, and I was surprised
when they handed me a huge mug of room-temperature dark ale. It
was very tasty, sweet but not too sweet. One mug of that ale, and I was
just about wasted.

One night, Ian, my new friend, reached into his pocket and pulled
out what looked like a huge cigar. I asked him what it was, and he said
it was a blunt of hashish. I had no idea what he was talking about. He
said it was like pot, only stronger. We smoked it at his place, and I was
so sleepy that I could hardly keep my eyes open. We had gone to a pub
before that, so I was wasted.

Needless to say, we ended up in bed, and all I remembered him
saying was "Wow, it is so much better when you really want to." The
next morning, I was so embarrassed, but he acted like everything was
good. He asked me to a concert to see a famous band, and I was excited.
I was waiting for him to pick me up, and he didn't show up. I was very
angry, and the next day, I went to his house and confronted him. He was
so nonchalant about the whole thing that it made me even angrier. He
told me he really liked me but knew that I was going back to the United
States and didn't want to miss me. I believed him, but I still felt cheap
and used. I found out later that he had fallen for another American,
and when she left, he was heartbroken, so I guess he was just trying to
keep that from happening again.

We started our first rotation in school at the hospital in a little
town not far from where I was living. We were working with mentally
challenged children. We learned how to do specific games with them
and taught them skills that were within their level of learning. We

interacted with them in a playful yet instructional nature. I enjoyed being with them, but at the same time, it made me sad. Looking back, I didn't know if it was because I was too young or just got too involved and close to them.

The second rotation was in a special hospital for paraplegics and quadriplegics. Paraplegics had paralysis of the lower half of their bodies, including both legs. Quadriplegics had complete paralysis of the body from the neck down. Therapy could be done as far as physical therapy, and other forms of treatment have been used where the therapist could use electrodes to stimulate the patient's muscles and give them an optimal workout.

At first, I was totally freaked out. It made me sad to see all those people, young and old, just lying in bed unable to move or sitting in wheelchairs. Some of them could at least move their arms, but all I could feel was pity. I thought about how I always took it for granted that I could walk and use my arms. I began to look at life with a different perspective and thank God for my arms and legs that I could use normally.

The guys kept telling me how pretty I was. In England, they say "bonny" instead of pretty. It made me feel kind of awkward at first. I tried to interact in a normal manner but didn't want to flirt. I was supposed to be a student professional. If I had been older, I could have handled the situation better.

I would never forget a lady in about her fifties looking up at me and telling me in a very mournful voice that she had fallen down five stairs and she never walked again. Her eyes were full of tears and I could feel her desperation. Every time I see someone on a roof or a ladder, I think about her. We have stairs at our house now, and I make sure they are well lighted.

I warn people who are using ladders or who are working on a roof to be careful. It made such an impression on me.

God bless those special people who overcome their handicaps and also those people who can work with the handicapped. There is a special place in heaven for them. I left my internship questioning myself if I was in the correct field. I had too much sympathy for them.

Since I was already in England, I asked my parents if I could stay a little longer and travel Europe. They were so giving, and I felt so blessed when they said yes. There was one stipulation, though; my brother,

Brad, went with me. I didn't want him to at first, but I was glad he did. We had a few sibling squabbles, but basically, we got along well. It was fun to get to know him again since we had been apart during our college years. He went to a university in Florida, while I was in Colorado.

Since we were already in England, we decided to go to all the tourist spots first. We saw Big Ben, Buckingham Palace with the stone-faced guards, Stonehenge with the "hanging stones," Cambridge University, and the beautiful cathedrals and museums. The two-story buses were fun to ride also.

We stayed in five-dollar hostels, which were like big dorms and also got a Eurail pass, so we could catch a train ride when we didn't feel like walking or hitching a ride. Most of the hikers were around our age, teens through twenties. There were kids from everywhere, and we met so many people just going from place to place.

I was surprised when the Canadians would get very upset if someone thought they were Americans. I wondered what their problem was. I didn't realize they didn't like Americans or why.

Before we left England, we went to a concert and they were fantastic. The lead singer was dancing all over the place, and you could smell pot everywhere. I started to get a little concerned when two English guys tried to start a fight with Brad for some unknown reason. Brad had long blond hair and looked like a hippie, but so did most of the kids there. I told him to ignore them because we really didn't need to get into trouble in a foreign country. They kept making rude remarks to him, and he told them he was a second-degree black belt in karate, and then they quieted down, thank God. We went to Amsterdam. It was beautiful there, with flowers everywhere. We met a very nice young local couple, and they invited us to stay at their place for three days. They showed us around and were very hospitable.

Brad and I were just walking around when we ended up in the red-light district. I saw these women sitting in individual glass cubicles and wondered who they were and why they were just sitting there like that. Then someone told me they were prostitutes showing themselves off, waiting for business. Brad said he wanted to go have some fun with one of them, and I said, "Absolutely not. Think of the diseases you could get from a prostitute." I didn't know if he really would have gone through with it or not.

The Anne Frank House was cool to see because we had both studied about her in high school. Also, the Van Gogh Museum was very interesting and, of course, Dam Square. We spent the night at another hostel and decided to go to Berlin.

Wow! It was hard to believe that people lived in such a militaristic lifestyle. It really made me think about our freedom at home. We were in a long line passing guards with machine guns while we waited to see the infamous Berlin Wall. The bombed old buildings were still standing next to the newly built ones.

We went to Auschwitz and saw the ovens where the Nazis burned the Jewish people. It was a horrific sight, and just thinking about it made me sick. Cast-iron statues of insanely thin people were scattered here and there. I was so glad to get out of there.

Austria and Switzerland were beautiful, with the majestic mountains everywhere. The Matterhorn in Zermatt, Switzerland, was awesome. It was the most famous peak in the Alps. We also went on a tour of the salt mines in Salzburg, Austria. We had to wear a black outfit and hat to protect us from the salt particles and sat on a little open train, which was fun. We ended up camping in tents that night near the Matterhorn with a bunch of other campers from all over Europe. It was like a big party.

Italy was next. It was so awesome. Florence had bridges of beautiful jewelry and leather goods just asking to be bought. The statue of David from the Bible was there. I was totally in awe to be able to see it. Of course, I had to buy a small statue of him as a souvenir. The old cathedrals had outrageously beautiful stained glass and high ceilings, which gave such a holy atmosphere for everyone.

We toured Venice, and it was even better than everything I had read about it. The gondolas were so much fun. The ice cream and the pizzas were superb. I slept in a convent with five Swiss girls one night, while Brad camped out. One of the other highlights for me was seeing the Leaning Tower of Pisa. I just lay on the ground on my back and watched the tower for hours. Brad and I took a nap there.

We went to Paris and saw the Eiffel Tower. We climbed as far up as we could. It was so cool to actually be on the Eiffel Tower. We also went to the infamous Louvre and saw the *Mona Lisa*. These were the highlights of Paris for me. The countryside was beautiful also.

Brad lost his passport in Spain. He left it in the bathroom, and when he went back to get it, it was gone. He had to stay in Madrid for three days to get the new one cleared. I left him and met a guy from South Africa and another from Poland. We had fun just learning about each other's countries and camping out.

After Brad got his new passport, we met a young couple from Greece. They had their own small yacht and offered to take us home with them to Crete, which was the largest island in Greece. I was so excited. I guess they thought it was cool to take us home with them too. The water was crystal clear blue, and the food was out-of-this-world delicious. We ate lots of baklava and moussaka. While we were eating at one restaurant, one of the dancers was dancing while holding the corner of a table in his mouth. I was mesmerized. I didn't know how he did it without breaking all his teeth. We thanked our friends for being so hospitable, and we exchanged addresses, with an offer to come see us anytime. After that, we made a quick trip back to Athens to see the Acropolis, and then our time was running out.

It was good to get back to the good ole United States of America. We had a wonderful experience for which I was very thankful for. I know my parents were glad we got home safely. The way Europe is now, I would be very hesitant to let my kids do what Brad and I had done.

When I went back to the University I attended and thought about my experiences during my residency in the hospital, I had to be honest with myself and admit that I really did not want to have a career in recreational therapy for the handicapped. I wasn't sure what to do because I was almost finished with my bachelor's degree.

I decided to talk to my pastor, Dr. D., about putting out a fleece, which meant that I wanted to carefully study my situation for indications of God's leading. Dr. D. agreed, and we both prayed about it. I was concerned about Dr. D. because he had gained a lot of weight since I had last seen him. I had always admired him and was thinking that, if he didn't lose some weight, he might develop diabetes. Even then, I was thinking like a nurse. I had heard my dad talk about different diseases while I was growing up and knew that diet and exercise were very important in staying healthy. Later, I found out that he passed from diabetic complications. It made me sad.

I decided to go back to the university closer to home and finish my degree. I only had two semesters left and thought maybe I could do something different with it than what I did in my residency. I moved into the sorority house just to see what it would be like and also to meet some more girls.

I did not fit in at first because, after being in Colorado for two years, I had basically turned into more of a hippie. I didn't wear any makeup while I was traveling Europe and didn't shave my legs or underarms all summer. I had hippie clothes, and I wore a headband around my long blond hair.

The girls were actually surprised I had a weighing scale in my room to watch my weight. I had always been somewhat vain. I was still mainly a vegetarian. In Europe, Brad and I practically lived off fruit and cheese in between real restaurants.

Gradually, I started dressing more like a Florida girl again instead of a Colorado girl. I made some good friends there and decided to move out. I moved into an apartment with one of my sorority sisters and two of her friends from high school.

There were four of us girls living in an apartment complex that was considered one of the wildest places to live. I was looking out the window one night, and there were a bunch of rednecks skinny-dipping in the pool at the complex. They were having so much fun. It was comical. My roommates were very conservative, but we all got along well together.

I decided I wanted to work part time and got a job at the local tennis shop near campus. I learned how to string rackets and met a lot of cute tennis players. I worked with a guy who was a twin named Ron and another girl named Bobbie. They were both students and fun to work with.

One day, this blonde-haired, blue-eyed, very tanned guy came in. I wanted to go out with him, so I flirted with him a little, and he asked me out. He was a little bit shy at first but soon was talking all the time. He told me he was from Upstate New York. I wasn't sure what that meant, but I knew it wasn't New York City. He had gone to school on a football scholarship at the University of New Mexico, where he was the quarterback. Unfortunately, he got a knee injury and had to drop out. His grandmother lived in Florida, and so did his aunt, so he decided to go to the university and played on the tennis team.

Before he did all this, he was drafted at eighteen years old, back when the draft was mandatory, to fight in the Vietnam War. He was a Green Beret, so they made him stay there for sixteen months.

He told me the kids were so scared fighting in the war that a lot of them smoked pot just to cope. The bad thing, though, was that whoever was on watch for the rest of them wasn't totally in control of the aggressive behavior of the enemy, and many of them died because of it. Landon, my new friend, said he never smoked pot. He was one of the men who scouted the area ahead of time and had to have 100 percent control of his mind. He told me later that someone stole his green beret, and he was very upset about it. I could understand why. He admitted that many of the kids came home with post-traumatic stress syndrome, and most didn't get the help they needed.

Landon and I dated each other off and on for quite a while. I saw other guys in between but no one really seriously. Landon was very jealous, but I told him we weren't married so I could do what I wanted. I think part of his problem was that he never knew his father, and his mother was a kind of controlling, selfish bitch. Landon spent most of his time in private schools. He also had a wonderful Christian grandmother, whom he was practically raised by. She told me Landon's mother was like a cat with a new partner every day. She was a very independent lady, and I really admired her. She was also the president of the women's club in her community and played golf almost every day.

I also dated a Cuban law student, whom I had known when I went to the local university my first year. He was very smart and amusing to me, I guess because of his different culture. His friends were loud and loved to dance to Hispanic music. He told me he had loved me for a long time, but I just didn't feel that way about him. He was a good friend to me. We ended up in bed together once, and when I discovered how small his penis was, I was shocked. Actually, I was embarrassed for him and for me. I decided it was better if we didn't see each other again.

I went out for a while with another law student. He loved working on my Mercedes. This was my second one, and it was a beauty. He was very handsome and funny and made a joke of having to make special time to be with me because he had to study so hard in law school. I knew the law students did have to read a lot. I became fickle again and moved on. He was another one whom, after looking back, I thought that maybe I should have stayed with.

I met a cutie from South America who had a sweet little sports car. His father was vice president of a huge banana company known internationally. I walked into his room, and it was entirely wallpapered with posters of his dad's banana advertisements. It looked really cool. Needless to say, he was very spoiled and spent lots of money on me. He was one whom I should have stayed with, but I didn't want to live in South America.

I finally finished my four-year degree and got my BS. I was a little behind because I had lived with my parents for a semester in between Colorado and Florida. One of the girls I had lived with in the big house in Colorado called me and apologized about how mean they had been to me when I lived with them. I thought it was nice of her to admit it. I accepted her apology and told her I forgave her. My mother took it to heart, but I knew they were just jealous of me. I still had fun there.

My parents knew I was very concerned about working with handicapped people at that time. I cried when I told them about my experiences during my internship. I still wanted to be a nurse, and even though my dad was against it, he said yes. Once again, I was so thankful to have such supportive parents.

I had two choices. I could take three more classes of prerequisites to get into the local university Nursing School or get right in at the Junior College, which is now a four-year college. I really didn't want to take three more extra classes because I was anxious to start nursing school.

Nursing School Begins

NURSING SCHOOL WAS VERY DIFFICULT. THEY SAY that half of nursing students don't finish because they don't like it or because it is too difficult scholastically. Also, I had a hypochondriac in my class who thought that she had every single disease that we studied. It was kind of sad but comical at the same time.

I was rather intimidated at first. The thought of sticking a needle into someone was very scary for me. We practiced on oranges and then on dummies. The more I did it, the easier it got. Shots in the arm were easier than in the butt. You had to be sure you shot them in the upper outer quadrant so as to miss a nerve.

IV therapy was quite difficult, depending on the type of veins that the patient had. We practiced on dummies. Thank God my first patient I had to put an IV in had big veins that didn't roll, and he was very patient with me. I was really pretty good at it.

To catheterize someone was a challenge, especially the little old women. It was difficult to find the right "hole," but I didn't like to catheterize men either because they always complained, and they were probably a little embarrassed. When I had a good-looking young patient, we were both embarrassed.

I was blessed to have two older women in my class whom I got along with well. They were always together and went out of their way to help me. Every time I said I wanted to quit, they would encourage me to stick with it. Looking back, I think they were lesbians but they never were improper with me. I was so thankful that God put them in my pathway.

My favorite class was anatomy and physiology. I was so fascinated about the body and how all our organs worked together to keep us functioning correctly, but we had to do our part by eating healthy and exercising. I already loved to exercise, but I could have eaten healthier. My teacher was a young guy who made the class interesting, and I made an A in it.

We started our first clinical rotation at the VA hospital there. My first patient was a little old man who had to stay in a wheelchair. I took him outside to be in the sun and get some fresh air. He seemed very appreciative, and when I took him back to his room, his roommates told me I was the only nurse who had been able to get him to leave his room and go outside. It made me feel good that I at least helped him emotionally. I had to catheterize a cute young patient there also, and it was embarrassing for both of us. Some of the duties of being a nurse could put you in situations you didn't want to be in.

We also did a rotation at a clinic in family practice. I found it interesting because we got to work with people of all ages, and most of them were not extremely ill. There were more medical students there, and we had a chance to interact with them more than at the VA hospital.

One of them asked me out. He wasn't really my type, but he was easy to talk to and seemed very smart. He told me his father was a doctor and an alcoholic. He told me he didn't drink because while he was growing up, his father used to get drunk and throw furniture all over the house. I felt sorry for him and couldn't imagine having a father like that.

We went out to dinner a few times. I had two beers, even though I knew he didn't drink. Alcohol always relaxed me, probably too much that night. We ended up at his place and in bed together. He told me he felt like he was with a prostitute. I didn't know if he was trying to compliment me or not, but it made me feel very uncomfortable and ashamed. I realized he probably had not had much experience with women. It also made me feel very guilty for being with him like I was corrupting him, the same way I felt about my friend who smoked the joint every morning before school when I was a freshman.

I was glad we met, though, because he noticed a mole on my arm and told me I should have it checked out. I knew he was smart and obviously very observant. I went home that weekend and told my dad what he had said. I got an appointment with my dad's doctor friend who had asked me out earlier. He was a general surgeon. He ended up cutting out a melanoma from my arm.

God saved me again. It was only a level 1. They can go up to level 4. Thank God they got all of it. If I hadn't met Jim, the med student, I might not be alive now. His quick, knowledgeable eye saved my life. When I got back to school, I made sure I thanked Jim for saving my life. We remained good friends after that. Dad had a very kind friend who owned a lot of land in real estate and was also in construction. We used to play tennis together. He visited me every day when I was in the hospital.

Another rotation we did was in the burn unit. I knew immediately that I would never want to work there. A husband/wife team of truck drivers was in a serious traffic accident, and their truck caught on fire. The wife's entire body was burned, and her husband died.

When we first walked in, all you could hear was this loud, agonizing moaning. We walked up to the patient who was lying there, and I was horrified by what I saw. That poor woman did not look like a human being. She looked like a big huge hunk of pink sausage. Her face had been burned off, and she was obviously in severe pain. I was sure they were giving her all the pain meds that they could. I couldn't help but think what kind of life she would have if she ever got out of the hospital. Sometimes I think it is just better to go to heaven than to have to live like that.

I also noticed that there was only one nurse and one doctor there. They were both very attractive, and it was noticeable to me that they were definitely closer than co employees. Stressful situations often brought out the need to relieve the stress. I think that might be one reason why doctors and nurses become attracted to each other while working under the stress that occurs in the hospitals or other medical facilities. I would definitely learn more about this later.

I had met a guy who was a clerk at the VA hospital when we rotated there. He was working and going to school at the University. He was studying pharmacy. He and I would talk occasionally while I was there. He called me one night and asked me out. We went to a little bar that had good music, and we really hit it off.

He was half American Indian, his mother being full-blooded Seminole. He was very big, tall, and muscular because he worked out a lot. He had darker skin and was very attractive. We ran together and kayaked down some of the local springs and rivers. We had a lot in common, except he liked me better without makeup. He liked the natural look. By then, I was back to being a prissy jock, and I told him he was just going to have to accept the fact that I liked wearing my makeup.

We went to our favorite little restaurant one night, and I, of course, drank some wine that night. He could drink a lot and eat a lot. His body was so awesome, and he had the biggest equipment I had ever seen, personally and professionally as a student nurse. He was so mellow and considerate; it was easy to fall for him. I almost didn't want him to touch me, though, because I was sore the whole next day.

One thing led to another, and I ended up getting pregnant. I didn't go on birth control because I kept thinking that I could control myself, but it was obvious that I couldn't. I always got too carried away emotionally and physically, especially when I drank. I was too young and stupid to make better decisions and kept meeting guys everywhere I went. No excuses for my mistakes would ever make it right.

I was devastated. I knew it was my fault, but when my period was late, I prayed to God that I wasn't pregnant. I sinned just one too many times, and this time, I got caught. Dakota, my baby's dad, wanted to get married. He said the same thing happened to his sister, and they got married, and she and her husband still managed to get through pharmacy school like he wanted to. He said they were still happily married.

The problem was that I didn't love Dakota that way, and I knew it. I didn't want to get married just because I was pregnant. I was just so messed up about how I related to men. I didn't know how to handle the attention in a mature way, especially if I was drinking or smoking pot. If I had to do it over again, I would have never drunk or smoked, but now I was paying the price.

I had to tell Dakota the truth about how I felt about him. It broke both our hearts when I decided to get an abortion. The doctor who did it was a nice-looking young OB/GYN resident, making extra money, I guess, at the local abortion clinic. I felt so bad and guilty about the whole thing, and I knew God wasn't happy with me and my choice, and neither was I. I was too immature to just go ahead and have the baby, and I could have put it up for adoption later if I wanted to. Needless to say, Dakota and I were finished.

Landon found out about it, and he was raving furious. He always had a very aggressive, jealous side and would throw me around. We went to the beach, and he practically raped me in his car. I was concerned that someone would see us, but I felt like I kind of deserved it. I was just so messed up. I told Landon I wanted to be with other people, but he was very possessive. His ex-girlfriend told me that he was a psycho freak, but I thought she was just trying to get him back. In actuality, he had post-traumatic stress syndrome from Vietnam. Every time it would thunder, if he was sleeping, he would wake up and freak out like he was in the war again.

I continued to study very hard in school. I was studying late one night, and someone knocked on our apartment door. It was the guy I had met in Aspen and had visited in Minnesota. I hadn't seen or heard from him for a while, but I remembered how cold it was out there. Even though he was handsome and well educated, he just wasn't my type. He and his friend were traveling in a huge camper and he wanted to come in. I told him I was in the middle of studying for a test, and I didn't have time to talk. I felt rude, but I shut the door.

I finally graduated from nursing school with a 3.7 average. I was so happy with my accomplishment, and my mom surprised me with a graduation gift. She had planned a trip to Japan and Thailand for both of us to go together. I was so excited. My mom loved to travel and so did I.

We stayed in Hawaii for a stopover for three days. The water was beautiful, and the food was delicious. We ate a lot of fish and sweet potatoes. Also, kalua pig was similar to our pulled pork with lots of pineapple. I almost missed the plane to Japan, though, because I met this cute guy, we got stoned together, and I lost track of time. My mom was very upset and rightly so. The flight to Japan was so long, just like the one to England had been. It was worth the wait, though.

My father and brother were interested in bonsais. Bonsais are dwarfed ornamentally shaped shrubs or trees in small shallow pots. I have two on my front porch. When they had gone to Japan for karate, they had become interested in them. Everywhere I looked while we were in Japan, there were beautifully and precisely trimmed gardens; even the big trees were perfectly shaped.

The people there were so friendly. They all wanted to take my picture. I felt like a movie star. I think it was because of my long blonde hair, and everyone there had dark hair. My mom was happy too because they thought she was my big sister.

The food was really good also. We ate lots of sushi; ramen, which was egg noodles in a salty broth; tempura, which was a light and fluffy batter that they use with seafood and vegetables; and mandarin oranges, which were my favorite. We took tours in Tokyo and rode the rickshaws. It was fun to see the ladies in their kimonos. Mostly, the older ladies wore them.

Then we went to Thailand. Mostly, I remember the huge statues of Buddha and the Buddhist priests walking around in their orange robes. I couldn't understand how the people could actually worship a statue of Buddha. It boggled my mind.

The opals and emeralds were very inexpensive there. My mom and I both bought a princess ring, which was a ring stacked with rows of both gems. They also had very different and exotic fruit there that I had never seen or heard of. They had custard apples, that you rip in two with your hands and eat the insides with a spoon; rambutan, that looked like hairy strawberries; dragon fruit; pomelo, similar to a sweet grapefruit; jackfruit, that grows up to massive sizes of eighty pounds; mangosteen; and many others. It was incredible.

We also made some nice friends on the tour and stayed in five-star hotels. It was a great trip with lifelong memories. In fact, I ended up taking care of one of the friends we made on the trip when I worked at a Memory Loss unit for Alzheimer's residents. Of course, she didn't remember me, but I remembered her. She was such a sweet lady.

When I got home, I decided to get a job at the teaching hospital near where I had gone to nursing school. This hospital was known all throughout Florida and the United States as being one of the best for unusual or complicated cases. There were over nine hundred expert physicians and more than eight thousand skilled nursing and support staff there.

Needless to say, that place was crazy busy, but I thought it would look good on my résumé. They had patients from everywhere with rare diseases and severely traumatized bodies. There were doctors, residents, interns, medical students, nurses, nursing students, and assistants all working with the same patients. Half the time, I couldn't even find the chart because I didn't know who had it.

It was very stressful working there. It was also very distracting having so many good-looking, smart young men everywhere to work with. We were right in each other's faces. One of my childhood friends was a nurse there and was dating one of the residents. He was arrogant, nice-looking, and a real dog—typical. She finally got smart and left the relationship. I was sure it didn't take him long to find another unsuspecting victim.

The worst for me there was walking into a room full of spina bifida babies. These babies were born with a defect that involved the incomplete development of the spinal cord or its coverings. Symptoms could sometimes be seen on the skin above the defect. They included an abnormal tuft of hair, a birthmark, or a protruding spinal cord tissue. They may have bed-wetting, muscular weakness, problems with their bowels, hunched backs, physical deformities, and many others. It made me really sad to see the severely deformed babies with their spinal cords sticking out of their backs. There were also so many of them in this one big room.

I also had to take care of five isolation patients at one time. It was so frustrating to have to put on a gown, surgical cap, mask, and shoe toppers; wash my hands; and then put on gloves for all five patients. As soon as I would get everything on, one of my other patients' light would go on. It was a nightmare. I didn't last long there.

Landon and I decided to get married. I knew I loved him, but looking back, I wonder if maybe I was just a little afraid of being completely on my own. We had been through so much together for several years, and it just seemed like the next thing I should do.

Life While Married to Landon

WE HAD A BIG WEDDING AT THE country club with 350 people. Most of them were my parents' doctor friends and Mom's social friends. My friends came, of course, the ones whom I had kept up with. Actually, most of my friends were already married. I was twenty-six years old, and Landon was thirty-one years old. It was a beautiful wedding, and my favorite pastor, Dr. D., married us.

After our honeymoon at the beach house of Landon's uncle, we moved into an apartment in my hometown and had some friends from high school living right next to us. I knew both of their parents, and they made great neighbors. I got a job at a nearby hospital, and Landon was a tennis pro at the local tennis courts/small country club in town. He actually made me a great tennis player and taught a lot of my mom's friends. We got along very well together. Landon seemed to calm down, and I vowed to stay committed to him for better or worse.

We bought two beautiful Persian cats and went to church next to our apartment where I had grown up in. We went to the couples' Sunday school classes and met a lot of young couples through the church. We saw my parents often, and my brother lived on the other side of the lake.

I started out working on the medical/surgical floor at the hospital, and I hated it. It was overcrowded, with patients' beds in the hallways and with no organization at all. I went to the director of nursing for the hospital, and she was a kind older lady, who said she had a position for me on a smaller floor. It was the neurosurgical floor with a few overflow medical patients.

We had a lot of patients with back injuries, neck injuries, head trauma, brain hemorrhages, CVAs, and seizures. One guy there had his butt cut off by an airboat, which really freaked me out. I felt sorry for him. A really pretty young girl came in one night from drunk driving. She was talking up a storm, but she didn't realize that she would probably never walk again. It made an impression on me about drinking and driving.

We had a young patient there in his twenties with a tracheostomy. His parents were always there. Trach care was not one of my favorite things to do, but I tried my best to look professional in front of them. I felt sorry for the whole family involved.

I saw my first patient die there. She was a sweet little old lady who had cancer. She was another overflow medical patient. She was slowly breathing with her mouth open, and then she was gone. I became so aware of how fragile life is. They came in with the bag, and she was gone.

I got my taste of doctors too while I was there. Most doctors whom I worked with were older. One of them was Scottish, and every holiday, he would dress up in his kilt and play the bagpipes for the patients. They loved it, and so did the nurses. He was a kind man, as well as a very smart doctor.

I accidentally gave the wrong medicine once. It wasn't anything threatening, but I was so afraid to tell him. He looked at me and said, "You will never make that mistake again, will you?" I was so relieved that he didn't yell at me and make a big deal about it. It made me like him even more.

There was one good-looking younger doctor who came to the floor for his medical patients. He was a huge flirt with all the nurses, and later, I found out that he married one of them, and they became part of a swingers group. I thought switching spouses only happened in the movies. Apparently, there were quite a few of them in town. I didn't understand the fun in that at all.

The male orderlies were fun to work with and helped us with the heavier patients. All in all, I liked most of the nurses I worked with. The head nurse was kind of weird and had a huge crush on the Scottish doctor. She made it very obvious, and it was kind of embarrassing for me to watch her make an idiot out of herself.

Landon decided he didn't want to be the tennis pro at the club anymore. One of my childhood friends got him a job in sales. Her dad owned a multimillion-dollar food-distributing company. He was our neighbor, who owned a Ferrari and a Mercedes. I would hear him going to work every morning at five thirty. Landon was very people oriented and quickly got a raise and a promotion.

We had to move to Miami, so I had to quit my job. We said good-bye to my parents and moved into a high-rise apartment building. We could hear the people next door constantly fighting; the woman would scream while the man threw her around, and she would hit the wall between us. I wanted to move.

We moved to a smaller quieter duplex closer to the beach. It was much nicer, and we had a fun young couple who lived next to us. The guy's parents had a lot of money. He worked for his dad, and it was obvious that he was a spoiled kid. His girlfriend was always showing me what she had bought at the designer stores at the mall. I wasn't envious at all. She was just amusing to me, and I felt like she was using her boyfriend for his money.

Landon and I were getting along pretty well. We both worked long hours and would both get home at different times. I had late hours at the hospital and was pretty tired when I got home. He rode around in his car all day, making sales calls. Sometimes he would wake me up in the middle of the night to have sex, and I was half asleep. I think if he had waited at least till morning, our sex life would have been better.

I woke up one morning, and Landon was masturbating in the shower while I lay there and watched him. He had left the bathroom door open. I was definitely caught off guard and wondered what was going on. I should have said something right away, but I let it slide. I guess I should have gotten into the shower with him, but it kind of ticked me off that he didn't come get me first.

I got a job at one of the local hospitals there, on the medical floor of all places. I quickly made friends with some of the nurses. They were very friendly to me, and being new, I really appreciated them. I didn't realize at that time that several of them were having affairs with some of the married doctors who worked on our floor.

I had been faithful to Landon since we had been married, and even though I always wore my wedding ring, it didn't seem to make much of a difference with the men down there, especially the doctors at the hospital. I was honestly shocked at how brazen they were toward me. I had really taken my marriage vows seriously. Even when we lived in our first apartment, the young guys would hit on me at the pool, and I had my wedding ring on.

One day at the hospital, I was with a patient in his room and had just finished attending to an IV treatment. Just as I was leaving the room, two of my nurse friends pushed this attractive tall muscular dark-haired man right into me. I was so embarrassed and excused myself for being so clumsy. They told me he had been wanting to meet me, so they helped him along. He was one of the doctors who worked on the same hospital floor that I did.

He introduced himself once we were out of the patient's room, and I didn't know what to say. He asked me if I would join him for lunch at the cafeteria downstairs during my lunch break, and he would meet me there. I said okay quickly because I needed to get back to work.

We met for lunch, and he told me he was from further south and had a lychee fruit tree farm, which he liked to take care of. He also liked to work out, which was obvious. He had a great body with big muscular arms. He was very easy to talk to, but I felt a little guilty being with him. Even though my sex life with Landon was getting worse and worse, I was still married. Kent, the doctor, said he wanted to see me again, but I told him I would have to think about it.

When I got home, Landon was watching television. I fixed him some dinner, and I watched a movie with him. We talked a little while, but I just couldn't help but think about Kent. I hated myself for it, but Landon hardly ever wanted to be affectionate anymore, and when I tried to talk to him about it, he just kind of blew me off. I wondered if he was having an affair or what. One of my friends asked me if he might be gay. That was the furthest thing from my mind. I never figured out what the problem was.

Eventually, I said yes to Kent. He was politely aggressive. He took me to his office after work. He was so proud of it because he had just finished having it remodeled. It was very luxurious and had a beautiful view of the city from a huge picture window. He had his own little kitchen with a wine rack on the wall. He told me about each bottle of wine and its history. I knew hardly anything about wine.

He put some cheese and crackers on the table and poured two glasses of wine for us. I knew I should have said no, but he was so charming and good-looking and smart that he was hard to resist. I drank a glass of wine, and we talked for a while. Then I drank another glass of wine, and before I knew it, he was kissing my neck and then my lips and gave me a gentle hug. Oh, how I had missed this, especially since Landon had not been paying attention to me lately.

One thing led to another, and we ended up on the floor. I loved having him on top of me, but it was a disappointment. He lasted about two minutes, and then he apologized. He told me I excited him too much. I felt kind of weird, guilty, and awkward all at once. Just as we were leaving, I noticed a picture of a woman and two kids near the window. He didn't wear a wedding ring, but I asked him about the picture, and he said they were trying to stay together for the kids. He said one reason he had his office remodeled was so he could stay there overnight if he wanted. I didn't understand then because I didn't have children yet.

We went to his beach house a few times, and it was beautiful to be right on the water. We were getting closer, but I knew I couldn't see him much longer. I was married, he was married, and it wasn't right.

I decided to leave the floor so I wouldn't have to work with him as much. My two best nurse girlfriends were continuing their affairs with the doctors, and I really didn't want to be involved anymore.

I got a position where I floated the hospital. It gave me good experience working with different specialties. I worked on the urology floor, which smelled like urine all the time; the cardiac floor, where all the patients were nervous wrecks and made me anxious; the orthopedic floor, with little old ladies with broken hips and young kids with broken arms and legs; the intensive care units; and the ER, full of traumatic situations. I didn't want to stay on any of them. I was glad I found out what I didn't want to do. My favorite patient during the whole ordeal was a guy who had cat scratch fever. I didn't know there really was such a thing. He was so nice and complimentary. He told me I was the best nurse he had ever had and called me Miss America. He at least made me feel appreciated. Nurses worked really hard, and it could be very stressful.

The oncology floor was actually one of my favorite floors. Even though all the patients had cancer, they had a humbleness about them. I guess by the time they got to that point, they had time to think about their lives more.

There were two doctors who basically ran the floor. I liked both of them. They were about thirty, and both had good senses of humor. That really made a difference when you were working on an oncology floor. They were both kind of flirty but in a fun way.

One of the patients needed an IV for chemo. The head nurse handed it to me and told me to give it. I checked the label, and it was the same blue color as always. The pharmacist had sent it down, so I gave it. I went in to check on my patient and reread the label and realized it was the wrong chemo. There were two chemotherapies with the same blue color and almost exactly the same names except for one number. Being a new nurse on the floor, I had just assumed that the pharmacist and head nurse would have checked it also. I was horrified that the wrong chemo was hung. I immediately stopped it. Thank God not much of it had infused. I told the head nurse, and the pharmacist brought down the correct one. The doctor was cool about it and said it wouldn't have made any difference anyway.

Another time, I was giving CPR to a patient, an older man with no DNR ordered, and the doctor told me to stop. I was shocked. He said the patient was dying and that I should just let him go. I became so confused about life and death at that time. I guess the doctors who worked on the oncology floor had experienced so much more than I had that they had a different perspective on life and death than I did. Later on, after I was a nurse for many years, I understood where they were coming from.

One of my favorite patients was a sweet little old lady with terminal cancer. The doctor ordered these little brown balls, which I had never seen before. They were soft and about as big as a pea. They were THC pills. I didn't think it was legal, but the doctor ordered them, and I gave them. She told me they helped her sleep better, made her appetite better, and helped her pain. I thought, *Well, if it helps her that much, why don't they just make it legal for medical marijuana?*

The family was at her bedside when I gave them, and they knew exactly what was going on. She did rest more comfortably but eventually died. I had to leave the floor because I was getting too attached to some of the patients.

Landon got transferred to a beach town further north. It was perfect timing because the hospital I was working at committed Medicare fraud and was being investigated by the FBI. I got out of there before all the chaos started.

I loved the little beach town. It was very quaint, and I loved being so close to the beach. Landon and I were growing apart, but we still wanted to try to make it work. I was hoping the move would give us a new start.

We found a cute little house in a nice neighborhood with very friendly neighbors. One of the ladies who lived down the street brought us a cake and invited us to a neighborhood party. It was fun to meet everyone and their kids. Most of them were working moms, but some stayed home with their kids.

I got a job at the local hospital there. It was much smaller than the hospital I had worked at before. In fact, the whole town was much smaller, with a homey atmosphere. The beachside was beautiful, with quaint little shops along the beachside roads.

There was one doctor there who was very nice-looking and cocky. I knew right away that he was one of the dogs. I didn't pay much attention to him, but of course, he noticed I was a new nurse there and just had to introduce himself.

I didn't really like working there and was so pleased when an older doctor came up to me and asked me if I would be interested in working at his office. I said yes and was so happy about getting the opportunity to try something different than hospital nursing. The doctor's name was Dr. Silver. He was extremely smart and had so many books in his office that it looked like a waist-high maze. You could hardly get to his desk.

Landon liked his job, but he had to travel more. He was gone several days during the week, so I didn't mind working later hours at Dr. Silver's. The doctor would come into his office about 10:00 a.m., and we wouldn't get out of there till 7:30 p.m. sometimes.

The doctor from down south, Kent, kept calling me and wanted to get together. I told him several times that we were too far away distance-wise and that I was no longer interested in seeing him.

I really liked working in Dr. Silver's office. I got to meet a lot of people, and most of them were not seriously ill. Dr. Silver enjoyed teaching me also and gave us a lot of independence. I worked with another older nurse, Viv, who had worked with Dr. Silver for a long time. She and Dr. Silver were like two peas in a pod. She was very attractive for her age, with bleached white hair and beautiful skin.

We had a lot of medical salesmen coming in to see Dr. Silver. He was known as one of the doctors who would take time to talk to them. They all had different personalities and would amuse us. When Viv and I were busy with the patients, they would talk to Callie, the receptionist, until Dr. Silver was available.

By now, Landon and I were not close emotionally or physically at all. I talked to Dr. Silver about it. I thought of him as my surrogate dad. I told him about Landon not wanting to have sex anymore, and he told me maybe Landon was gay. The thought had never entered my mind, but some of my nurse friends had said the same thing.

Landon got transferred again. I didn't want to be married to him anymore. I decided to stay where I was and keep the house. He took the two cats rather than split them from each other, and we ended up getting a divorce. My parents were pretty upset at first. I didn't tell them about what a temper he had. He got really angry with me one night and strangled me. I had to go to work with bruises all over my neck. I tried to cover them up with a turtleneck, but it was still obvious. Everybody knew, even Dr. Silver. He told me it was better for my safety to stay away from him.

Starting Over Again

THERE WAS A GOOD PLASTIC SURGEON IN town, and I still had a huge scar on my arm from my melanoma. My sweet daddy paid for the plastic surgeon to make my scar smaller, and Dr. Silver gave me a medical leave of absence. My right arm was in a cast, but thankfully, I am left-handed.

One night, I heard some scratching noises outside my bedroom window. I got my gun out, cocked it, and was ready to shoot if someone tried to come through my window. I called my neighbor across the street, and he came over with his gun. He looked around the yard for me but didn't see anybody and said it was probably just a raccoon or some other animal. I was still waiting inside for him with my gun cocked, and he had to put the safety on for me because I couldn't with my cast on.

The next morning, I checked outside around my bedroom window, and there were two big shoe prints facing my window like they were trying to get in. That really scared me. I called the police told them what happened and asked them to please patrol the neighborhood at night for a while. They were very accommodating.

I decided to get a roommate so I wouldn't be in the house by myself. She was a tall athletic blonde, Lauri, and she had a cute boyfriend. He was always over there, though, and I got kind of tired of them, but it helped to have the extra money.

I met a guy who had his own private airplane. He had wild curly blonde hair and was very aggressive. When he asked me if I wanted to fly in his plane, I told him I get sick in smaller planes. He said he would fly very smoothly and that it would be fun. We packed a picnic basket and had a nice lunch and then went flying on his plane. He started doing flips in the air. I told him to quit, or I was going to throw up. He didn't believe me and said he would stop doing flips, but I asked him to land, or I was going to throw up. When we finally landed, I puked all over the back of his plane. Thankfully, we had put our picnic basket behind us, and most of the vomit landed in the basket.

I saw him for a while but tired of him also. I found out later that he was using his plane to smuggle marijuana in from the border. I had set him up with a friend of mine, and she was called into court to testify. I felt bad about the whole situation because neither one of us knew anything about it. I could have gotten into a lot of trouble because of him. God saved me again.

I started hanging around two of the nurses at the clinic where Dr. Silver's office was. It was a multispecialty clinic. These nurses were not a very good influence on me. They loved to party, and they were single. Dorrie had been involved with somebody in the Mafia and married six times. Later, we found out she had a fake nursing license and wasn't even a nurse. She was a real character but fun to be with. Tracy was dating one of the doctors at the clinic who was married. I didn't know all this when I first met them.

They invited me to a party at the snobby country club. I felt a little out of place since I didn't know anyone. There were a lot of people partying, and I recognized some of the doctors from the hospital that I had worked at briefly. I was getting kind of bored, and just as I was leaving the club, this attractive tall blue-eyed man came up to me. He said, "I wondered where you went." I didn't know what he was talking about. He told me that he had seen me at the hospital, and then I disappeared, and he wondered where I had gone. He caught me way off guard.

He told me he had wanted to introduce himself but never got a chance. I told him I had left the hospital to go work for Dr. Silver and how much I liked it there. We talked for a while and ended up on a private yacht with some other people, mostly doctors and nurses. Everyone there was sworn to secrecy, I found out later. He was very nice, and he wined and dined me, and we went fishing on his boat.

Then one night, he took me to his house. I assumed he wasn't married. We really didn't talk about it. When we got there, he told me his wife was out of town for the weekend, and they really weren't getting along. I had heard that line before.

We ended up in his bed, and I felt so guilty. I told him I would never go there again. The last thing I remember as I was leaving was seeing a plate of cookies in the kitchen, which his wife had probably left out for him. What a jerk. I told him I didn't want to see him again, and he whined like a little baby. He was really weird about his penis too. He always wanted me to call it a cock because for some reason, that turned him on.

I was so glad I liked my workplace. Dr. Silver was so good to us. He took us out to lunch and gave us expensive gifts from his wife's antique store, and we were paid the highest of all the nurses in the clinic. He was also very kind and trustworthy. One of the nurses started a rumor that Dr. Silver and I were having an affair. I laughed when I heard that and went straight to the source. I told her how ridiculous that was and why she would even bother to make up such a gossipy story.

I went out with one of the salesmen who called on Dr. Silver. He was a runner like I was, and we ran together on the beach. He told me to always keep my toenails short so as not to get "black toe." Apparently, the pressure on your toenails when you are running can actually cause your big toenail to turn black if it is too long. I learned something. He told me he just wanted to be friends, and I said I did also. It impressed me when he told me he wanted to always be faithful to his wife. That was the way it should be.

Some of the nurses and I went to a local restaurant/bar that was popular in town. They served great seafood, and they had outside seating. We had been there for a while, and I was getting a little bored and decided to go home. I started walking to my car. I had another Mercedes but a different model from my first one. Just as I started up my car and was leaving the parking lot, all of a sudden, this tall figure stood in front of my car and wouldn't get out of the way. I honked my horn and asked him to move.

He came up to my window and told me he had been watching me from the bar and wanted to meet me. I thought, *Oh my gosh, I've heard this before.* It was getting darker, and I wanted to leave, but he stuck his head in my window, and I could see his face better. He was the most gorgeous guy I have ever seen to this day. He looked like a model I had seen advertising a men's cologne. He was tall and had chiseled features, thick long dark hair, and the most beautiful eyes. He was oozing with sexiness.

I told him I really needed to get home, but he got in the passenger seat and wouldn't get out. I asked him where I could drop him off, and he asked if we could just go for a walk on the beach. We went to another little secluded bar on the beach and then walked in the moonlight. I could see that he was younger than I was, but it was difficult to estimate how much younger. He was easy to talk to, and after our walk, I dropped him off at the bar where we had met. He said he had come with some friends. He asked me for my phone number, and thinking I would probably never see him again, I gave it to him.

The next day, after I got home from work, he called me. He said he wanted to meet me at one of the local beach restaurants. I was a little nervous because I remembered how good-looking he was. When I saw him again, my heart skipped about ten beats. Why did he have to choose me? I always got into trouble when good-looking guys pick me first. I really wasn't ready for this emotionally.

I got a better look at him in the daylight, and honestly, I kind of felt like I might be robbing the cradle. He looked so much younger than he did the night before. He was with some of his friends and they kept staring at me. I felt very uncomfortable around them and told him I would feel more comfortable if it was just the two of us.

We got away from the crowd and talked awhile. His name was Carson. He looked like the perfect model for anything he put on his gorgeous body. He told me he had just gotten off football practice at the private school there. I said, "The private high school?"

And he said, "Yeah, I didn't want you to know I'm eighteen years old." I flipped out. I was thirty years old at that time and had never even thought about being with an eighteen-year-old. If he hadn't been so gorgeous, I would have never seen him again. He said he knew I was a little older, but that didn't make any difference to him.

I took him home with me, and we ended up doing it on the couch. He was even more gorgeous without his clothes on. I knew it was wrong for me to be with him. I just wished that he had been older. I told him I really liked him, but the age difference made me feel awkward. He wanted to continue to see me, but I introduced him to a pretty younger girl his age, and they seemed to get along well. I also gave him my fifth-grade Bible. I felt flattered that he was attracted to me, but I felt more like his big sister.

I met a professional baseball player at a bar in town while I was out with some of my nurse friends. His team had spring camp there. He was one of the older players on the team but had a great record and was well-known nationally. His name was Derek, and he was very handsome and well-mannered. He was the pitcher of the team. I went over to his apartment, and his roommate was there. He was a real jerk and told me that the team would have parties and see who could bring the fattest and ugliest girl to the party. I told him that was disgusting, but he thought it was funny. Of course, the girls all realized what was going on once everyone arrived. Derek told me he didn't participate and agreed with me. We kept in touch for a while, but the distance made it difficult when he was in San Francisco.

I had a black girlfriend named Lena, who did EKGs at the clinic. She and I really got along well. She was funny and really into clothes like I was. She had a boyfriend named Hank, who was a pharmacist in town. One day, she told me at work that Hank had a friend who was one of the medical salesmen who called on Dr. Silver, and he wanted to go out with me. They had it all planned out that we would double-date with them. I didn't even know who she was talking about. I told her he would need to introduce himself, and I would make the decision if we would go out or not. I knew most of the salesmen, and they would have asked me out on their own. He must have been one of the few who didn't hang around and chat with us while waiting for Dr. Silver.

The next day, he came in to talk to Dr. Silver. He introduced himself to me, and I was pleasantly surprised. He was a very nice-looking guy. He was a tall blonde with blue eyes and a beautiful smile. I remembered him, but he was rather quiet compared to the older guys who came in. Most of the other salesmen were a lot more flirty. He said his name was Ted.

It was rather awkward talking to him at the office in front of everyone else. After he saw Dr. Silver, we managed to set a date up for that weekend with Lena and Hank. I gave him my phone number. It put a smile on my face. He looked a little bit younger than I was but not that much.

That Friday night, Lena, Hank, Ted, and I went to a nice restaurant in town. I expected Ted to be sophisticated and classy because he looked so nice in his suit at the clinic and acted like a gentleman. We all got along well, and Lena and I called ourselves the salt-and-pepper couples.

When we got ready to order for dinner, Ted said he wasn't hungry because he had just had a chili dog. I was so shocked that he would say that. I was used to being wined and dined when I went out on a real date. I didn't even bring any money with me because I thought Ted was going to pay for my dinner. After all, it was his idea to take me out.

I ordered the least expensive thing on the menu and told Lena I would need to borrow some money from her to pay for my dinner. Thankfully, Ted said he would pay for mine. It was awkward. My thoughts of him being sophisticated and suave went out the window. I guess I was just so wrapped up in how good-looking he was that I made inaccurate assumptions.

We went bar hopping after that, and Ted could really drink. He liked White Russians, and so did Hank. Vodka made me really drunk, so Lena and I just sipped on our margaritas, while the boys belted their drinks down. I was glad I had decided to drive my own car because I thought I might have to drive Ted home after seeing him drink so much.

We parted our ways, and we each went home. I didn't know if I would see him again, but I really liked him. I felt like he was attracted to me also. I had been with so many guys that I learned not to expect anything or to commit to anything. I knew I was still messed up in the relationship department, but I at least tried to be honest with whomever I was with. I still felt really guilty about how my marriage with Landon had fallen apart.

The next day at work, Ted came into the office, and we talked a little while till Dr. Silver came in at his usual late time. We had lunch together, and he asked me to meet him at his apartment after work. He showed me around, and I didn't think much of it. Then he told me he was only living there until his house was finished being built. It did kind of impress me that a twenty-seven-year-old was having his own house built. I was thirty-two years old now, and I would have traveled a little more rather than build a house at that age, but it did show motivation, which I really liked and still do.

He told me his mom was visiting from Ohio for a while, but she was with a friend for the weekend. We had some White Russians together at his place. Since this was his favorite drink, I thought I would try one, even though vodka was really too strong for me. They were really good, so I drank another one. He could always drink twice as much as I even wanted to.

We ended up in his bedroom. There was something different about Ted that I liked, besides the fact that he was so good-looking. He liked to work out at the gym and told me he was bored with his job and wanted a more challenging one. He also told me he had really wanted to go to medical school after college but put it on the back burner because it was so expensive. I was thinking that he could have gone instead of building a house, but I didn't know him well enough to say that.

When he told me he sold LSD during his college days to make some extra money, I didn't think anymore about it. I just assumed it was a passing phase. He said he and his friend quit selling because they were afraid they might get caught. It made me think of my roommate in Colorado who was on LSD and talking about how red the tomatoes were. I decided it was time to go home, so we parted our ways.

We went to the gym together, and he showed me some exercises to do with some weights. We also ran and started spending more and more time together. Dr. Silver asked me if I was just with him because he was so nice-looking. I laughed and told him that I would like him even if he was a pirate with a patch on one eye.

We were at his apartment one night when his mother wasn't there, and when we were in bed together, I had this strange feeling that I wanted to marry him. *He was so gentle and loving and was everything I wanted in a man*, I thought.

He took me home that night, and just as he was leaving, he looked at me and told me he just wanted to be friends. I said, "Fine with me. Don't ever call me again," and I meant it. The nerve of that guy. Who did he think he was? What a weirdo.

I was going home to visit my parents the next day, and when I got there, my mom said that some guy named Ted had just called asking if I was there. I couldn't believe that he called my parents' house after what he said to me. I really didn't want to talk to him. He called me while I was there and said he wanted to see me again. I was very leery of him at this point and wasn't sure if I wanted to see him again or not. I told him I would think about it while I was at my parents.

I decided to forgive him and give him another chance. We got back together, and he seemed more normal. He said he had just broken up with a girl who was an alcoholic and bulimic, and he was trying to help her. That was why he was hesitant to get involved with someone else so soon. He said his mother also told him it was too soon. That should have tipped me off then.

As I got to know him better, he showed me his new house that was finally finished. It was a really nice house in a middle-class neighborhood. There were pine trees all around the house, and when the wind blew, they whistled. I met some of the neighbors, and they were all very friendly.

Ted was very motivated, and for the first time since Landon, I really felt like I wanted to marry this guy. It was for a different reason also. I was older and not overly concerned about my future like I was when I married Landon. Everywhere we went, people called us Barbie and Ken, just the way they had called Landon and me Barbie and Ken. It was amusing to me.

His mother and older brother moved down from Ohio and moved into his house with him. From then on, we had absolutely no privacy. His mother, Nita, and brother, Anthony, were always there when I went to his house. His mom was always knocking herself out cooking for her grown boys, and Anthony did nothing but sit on the couch, watching television and drinking beer. Anthony was my age. He was nothing like Ted. Anthony was a little overweight and not very motivated. He also smoked, which has always bothered me.

Ted's father came down later after the house was sold in Ohio, and he found a place closer to the beach. Apparently, his mom didn't like his dad very much, and they stayed together because they were Catholic, and his mom was afraid to get a divorce. Ted's sister, Susan, was a nurse, and she had moved down to Florida first. She had helped Ted find his job in medical sales. She and I got along well, and she invited us to her house nearby. Her husband was an engineer and worked with one of the airline companies, so they got big discounts whenever they traveled.

Ted and I had been dating for about a year now. As I got to know him better, I realized he was a bit moody and more of an introvert than I was. We would go out drinking, and then he would liven up. We would fight about stupid things but would always make up. I was a spoiled doctor's kid, and he was a cop's kid. His dad, Ben, worked very hard, though, as a security guard after he retired from the police force.

We decided to get married, and I was scared. I talked about going away to Africa and be a missionary, and it would really frustrate Ted. Finally, I settled down and told myself that Ted and Landon were entirely different in many ways. I was definitely destined to realize just how much later on in my journey.

We had a small family wedding in a beautiful little chapel with stained glass windows all around us. I had a gorgeous wedding gown, and Ted looked so handsome in his tuxedo. The sunset was perfect while we had our wedding photos taken. Ted said he had prayed for the perfect sunset. That really warmed my heart. I was so in love with someone whom I thought was the perfect man for me.

Ted's family couldn't afford to help him pay for a honeymoon for us, so once again, my parents took us to Aspen. We had been going there ever since I was nineteen years old. It was like a family tradition. My brother was with his wife's family; otherwise, he would have gone also.

I knew it was kind of awkward for Ted at first, but I had spent too much time with his family since his mother and brother moved in with him. Thankfully, they had found an apartment near Ted's dad and were moving out while we were in Aspen. We had fun skiing, and Ted got to know my parents better. One night, my mom did a smelly huge fart, and it stunk up the entire condo. We had to leave for several hours while Mom aired it out. Needless to say, I was rather embarrassed, but he definitely got indoctrinated into my family's lifestyle.

The Beginning of My Journey with Ted

AFTER OUR TRIP, WE WENT BACK TO his house. I was so excited that we were finally going to have the house to ourselves without his mom and brother there. We walked into the house, and they had not moved out yet. I was very ticked off. Anthony had already told me about their apartment and how he had smoked a joint off the balcony.

Two weeks after we were married, they were still there. I couldn't understand what was wrong with them. I told Ted that it was past time for them to move. We had asked them to move earlier. I told Ted if they didn't leave that I was going to get the marriage annulled, and I meant it. Ted's mother had wanted us to get married in a Catholic Church, so I agreed to talk to a priest. When I finally realized they wanted me to get my first marriage annulled and include my friends answering personal questions about my marriage, I said no. What in heaven's name does a priest know about marriage? The Catholic priests weren't allowed to get married. Ted could see how upset I was, and they finally moved out.

It didn't take me long to figure out that Nita and Anthony had a codependent relationship. I had heard of "Mama's boys" before, but now I fully understood what it meant. Ted spent every weekend visiting his parents at their separate apartments, and frankly, I just didn't want to go over there every weekend, so I didn't.

It soon became a realization to me that Ted's father and brother were both alcoholics. They had beer cans all over the kitchen, and I just felt totally out of place. All they did was sit around and talk about Ohio, and it became very stressful for me. I wanted to be with my husband on the weekends. Why had Ted changed so when his family came down?

I started having problems with my skin breaking out because of all the stress I was under because of his family. I went to the doctor and he put me on an antibiotic. After taking it a few days, I developed a side effect of ringing in my ears. It was so loud that I thought there was an ambulance outside our window. It was driving me crazy.

Ted was calling on a doctor who was taking the same antibiotic that I was, and he told Ted that he had ringing in his ears also. Ted said his wife was not supporting him with it, and he ended up committing suicide. I had briefly thought about it, but my mother said it would have killed my father if I did something like that. I was just so desperate, so I understood why the doctor killed himself. It made me very sad and totally freaked me out.

I wrote to the pharmaceutical company and told them about the ringing in my ears and about the doctor killing himself because of it. They said they had no other complaints and did nothing to help me. I think the doctor and I got a tainted batch of the same medicine.

I heard about a faith healer who was coming to town. I remembered my Pentecostal church I had gone to in Colorado and had actually experienced the laying on of hands, speaking in tongues, and healing. I wanted to go. Ted was a bit skeptical, but he went with me. That meant a lot to me, and he knew how distraught I was.

When we got there, there was a group of people gathering around another person, speaking in tongues, and laying their hands on him. I was so ready to try this and had big faith that I would be healed. I met the faith healer ministers. They were a husband-and-wife team. I told them about the ringing in my ears and how I got it.

A group of people gathered around me and laid their hands on my head, my shoulders, and my back. They started praying in tongues, which I couldn't understand, but I knew it was in the Bible.

I started getting wobbly and felt like I was losing my balance. The people behind me told me not to worry and that they would catch me. I didn't know what they were talking about, but I took my high heels off anyway.

They kept praying, and I fell straight backward, and they caught me just like they said they would. I didn't know what had happened to me, but they told me that I had been slain by the Spirit, which was the power of the Holy Spirit. I was in total awe. I had absolutely no control while falling backward. It just happened, and if it hadn't happened to me, I wouldn't have believed it. Now I was a 100 percent believer in the power of the Holy Spirit to heal and being slain by the Spirit.

They told me to recite Ephesians 6:13–17 every time the ringing would start. Since it was a constant ringing, I quoted the Bible verses over and over again. The ringing stopped. I was so thankful and thanked the faith healers for saving my life. This Bible verse was ingrained into my brain. It talked about putting on the full armor of God. Put on the helmet of salvation, the breastplate of righteousness. Gird your loins with truth. Shod your feet with the preparation of the gospel of peace. Fight with the sword of the Spirit, which was the Word of God, and the shield of faith by which you extinguish every flaming dart the wicked one brings against you.

I went home, and Ted was truly amazed. He didn't understand what happened, but he knew it had worked. Every time the ringing would start, I would recite the verses, and it went away. The ringing got less and less, and the power always worked. Later in my journey of life, I have said these verses many times.

I told everyone at work what had happened. I was not sure if they believed me or not, but I didn't care because I knew it was *real*.

I continued to work at the clinic for Dr. Silver, and Ted continued with his pharmaceutical sales job. After about a year of marriage, I decided I wanted to have a baby. Ted and I were getting along well, and I was thirty-three years old. I was in good health and went to the gym almost every day. Since Ted was five years younger than I was, he didn't feel exactly the same way I did about having a baby, but he said okay. I had no problem getting pregnant. They put me under anesthesia because Ted and I both had herpes when we met, and we wanted to be sure that the baby was safe. I had my first C-section.

He was born with bright red hair, and my mom said she picked him out to be mine. I was born with red hair also. She said he was screaming the whole time she watched him through the nursery window, and he continued screaming for three months straight after he was born. I had to carry him in a baby sling in front of me everywhere we went. He loved the automatic swing inside and anything where he could move. It was difficult for him to be still.

We named him Mark, like in the Bible. I wanted my children to be raised in the church and know Jesus. The first night, we had him in a bassinet next to our bed. Ted complained that he was grunting like a pig and demanded that Mark and I go sleep in another room on the other side of the house. My feelings were hurt at first, but since I was on a six-week maternity leave, I felt like the least I could do was let Ted get his sleep.

Mark and I settled into our new room. He still cried all the time, and I kept him next to me while we were sleeping. I was breast-feeding him, and it was much easier that way. I looked at him one day, just lying there crying, and prayed to God to help me have more patience with him and for him to stop crying so much.

My mom and mother-in-law, who had never breast-fed their babies, told me I probably didn't have enough breast milk, and maybe I should start giving him a bottle. I stupidly listened to them although I liked breast-feeding Mark. There was a closeness there that only a mother who breast-fed would understand. He still cried even with the bottle, and I tried to breast-feed again, but my milk had dried up. I was very annoyed at both my mom and mother-in-law for telling me to quit, but I knew they were only trying to help. Lesson number one to all new mothers: go with your own heart's feelings no matter what anyone else tells you. Mark eventually grew out of his crying phase, which we later found out was because he was colic. Colic was usually caused by an abnormal amount of gas in the baby's intestines, and it makes the baby cry from the pain. I had tried some over-the-counter meds for him, but they didn't work that well.

Mark loved his juice, and one night, I couldn't get him to drink. He was rather lethargic. I took his temperature, and it was 104 degrees. We took him to the ER, and I was praying the whole time for God's help. They got his temperature down and gave us some medicines, and then we went home. I was so thankful my baby was okay. Our guardian angels were protecting us again.

Ted decided he wanted to make more money since we had started a family. He had a friend who was doing really well selling knee implant equipment. He told Ted he could use another salesman on his team, and Ted started working for him. The guys on the team had this ritual where they would wear sunglasses and go around saying, "Our future is bright." I thought it was comical, but at least they were positive.

We had to move to another city further north in Florida, where I had gone to nursing school. Ted was doing pretty well with his new job, but he found out that there was a lot of competition, and he would have to wait around for a while till the doctors could see him. He also had a large territory and would come home frustrated and tired.

There were several medical students and residents who lived in our neighborhood, and I made friends with their wives who had young children. We all enjoyed one another's company and had play days almost every day.

Mark was almost two years old and was the biggest kid around. He was so big that the other mothers started calling him a bully. He was just rougher because of his size, and one of the other kids was real tiny for his age because he had been born premature. The next-door neighbor was a girl, and even though we liked our kids playing together, Mark was just too rough for a girl. I was so happy when another kid moved into the neighborhood who was big and rough and tough like Mark. They became best friends.

I got pregnant again when Mark was a little under two years old. I started having contractions when I was at a women's social club meeting. I was in labor all night, and it was horrible. I didn't have to do that with Mark.

My obstetrician was gorgeous with very good bedside manner and had a good medical reputation. If I had known ahead of time that he was a big partier and cocaine user, I would have had another doctor deliver my baby. A friend of Ted's told us about him using cocaine. Thank God everything worked out.

Melissa, my second baby, was stuck in my rib cage, and he ended up doing a C-section at the last minute. I couldn't believe she was mine when he pulled her out and showed her to me. She had curly black hair and slanted eyes. I was glad I was awake during the whole procedure.

She was a great baby. Instead of crying all the time, like Mark had, she slept all the time. In fact, I couldn't wake her up one night and rushed her to the hospital. Just as we entered the ER doors, she woke up and started crying. I was so happy. I knew in my heart that God was with me. I had been frantic, thinking she had something drastically wrong with her. I was thirty-eight years old when I had her, and the doctor had given her a clean bill of health. God is so good.

Ted became increasingly frustrated with his job and realized that "the future wasn't quite so bright" as his friend had promised him. He quit selling knee implants and started a new job doing medical research. He enjoyed his new job, and the hours were much better.

Then we started talking about him wanting to go to medical school. His past desire to go was influenced by all our new friends who were medical students or residents. I talked to my dad about it, and he said he would give me more of my trust money to help us get through medical school. He told me he felt like it would be a waste of a good mind if Ted didn't go.

We were both getting excited about the idea, even though we knew it would be a long road and quite expensive, but we were both willing to make the commitment. By now, Ted was thirty-three years old, and most medical school students started at twenty-three years old. His age could work either for him or against him.

Ted studied really hard for the MCAT, which stood for Medical College Admission Test. He made excellent scores. He made a big poster with his scores written on it and hung it above his study desk so I could see it when I walked in. It was such a pleasant surprise, and I was so proud of him. He was very motivated, and his hard work had paid off.

Ted applied to several medical schools and got accepted to the school he really wanted to go to. We were excited because we thought maybe the other schools were biased against him because of his age. The recruiter at Ted's school was really cool, and his philosophy was that the older students were more committed, and he liked Ted anyway. He told Ted he would still have the opportunity to work for a long time after he got out of all his schooling. Oh, how life has a way of surprising us!

Our Big Move for Medical School

WE NEEDED TO LOOK FOR A PLACE to live, and since my dad was so kind and generous, he gave us money to buy the perfect house for us. It was a neighborhood full of kids and had a huge oak tree in the backyard. We had a wooden playhouse/fort built with a sandbox underneath it and a nice swing set. We were so happy there.

Mark and Melissa were getting older now, and Ted started medical school and loved it. He studied all the time. I put Mark and Melissa in a preschool near us so I could have some free time to go to the gym by myself. The first day, Melissa cried the whole time. I only left them there for a half day. I thought it would be a good way for them to meet some new friends and learn at the same time. They were there three days a week. The owner and I became good friends, and she told me Melissa was the most stubborn kid she had ever had and knew every single kid's name in the preschool. She soon got used to it after she made some good friends. Mark, of course, had no problem and made several good friends within a few days.

One of Mark's friends bit both his arms from his shoulders to his hands. When I picked him up that day, I was very upset. Gina, the owner, told me to tell Mark to bite him back, but it was our secret. Mark started biting him, and that was the end of the biting.

One of the little girls at the preschool had a very flirtatious father who kept telling me how pretty I was. His daughter was beautiful. They were Arab. She had dark skin and beautiful hair and eyes. One day, when he picked her up, he told me a famous rock star was in his car. I didn't believe him at first, but his daughter had been named after one of his songs. I wanted to go over and meet him, but I was too shy.

Mark went to the local elementary school when he turned five. He was still one of the biggest kids there. One day, on the school bus, one of the other kids was trying to bully him, and they got in a fight. Mark finally found his match. They became good friends, and his mother and I became good friends also. She was a pretty blonde and was married to a Hispanic guy. Later, after we moved, I found out they got a divorce, and her son was killed in a car accident at the age of nineteen years old. I felt so bad for her, but she was a very strong woman.

Another time at school, Mark got in trouble with another kid who made fun of him when he missed the toilet when he was peeing. Mark wiped his hands on the other kid who told the principal. She told me she had to call me, but she thought it was funny.

I was so happy just being a mom and was thankful that I got to stay home with my kids, thanks to my dad. We were always busy going to the children's museum, the zoo, the aquarium, and doing activities with the neighborhood kids. I tried to keep Ted involved with the kids as much as possible, but he had to study so much that it was difficult.

I found a very nice boutique with beautiful and unique clothes, shoes, hats, and jewelry. The two ladies who worked there became my good friends. I tried not to go in there, though, because it was so tempting. I always got complimented whenever I wore clothes from there. Later, I found out that one of them got hooked on painkillers because of her fibromyalgia. She was a beautiful redhead and always looked like she walked right out of a fashion magazine. I felt so bad for her because she had mentioned to me that her whole body hurt her.

I got pregnant again when I was thirty-nine years old. I was still in great shape and went to the gym all the time. I was so excited. Mark and Melissa were six years old and four years old and getting to be more independent. Ted was happy about it at first, but he came home one day from medical school extremely stressed out. He said he could hardly move his fingers and felt like he might end up in a wheelchair. He totally freaked me out. He had me believing that he was very ill. I began to get severe headaches, and I never got headaches before. They were so bad that I could hardly take care of the kids.

Ted told me it was probably from the pregnancy, and there might be something wrong. He said, since he might end up in a wheelchair, that maybe I shouldn't have the baby. That was not what I wanted to hear from him. I flashed back to the abortion I had when I was in nursing school and how sad it made me. I really wanted to keep this baby.

My headaches got worse, and Ted was still having difficulty moving his fingers. He said I might be taking care of the kids by myself while he was in a wheelchair. I was so unhappy, and I knew God didn't want me to have an abortion.

I finally had it done and cried the whole way there and for the next several days. The nurses there looked like they could feel my emotional pain. The doctor was older, who said he had six kids of his own, and it was too many. He was very cold and had no bedside manner. It was a horrible experience, and I was so sad. Ted said I did the right thing, but I knew I didn't and asked God to forgive me.

I ended up having a second melanoma found by one of Ted's medical student friends. They weren't going to biopsy it at first, but we insisted that they did. My first one had been atypical also. Thank God it was also a level 1. The doctor who took it off was a professor at the university, as well as a dermatologist.

Ted seemed to be getting better. He didn't complain about his fingers anymore or about how he felt like he was going to end up in a wheelchair. Remembering these facts made me think that maybe they were early symptoms of a disease that he would get later.

I still wanted to have another baby. Ted was more agreeable this time, and I got pregnant at forty-one years old. I prayed that God would help me get through the pregnancy with no complications. They put me on high risk because of my age but took me off because I was in such good shape. Going to the gym has always paid off.

I went to my favorite boutique, and they had clothes I could wear as my pregnancy progressed. I used a decorative brooch that I wore in the back of my dress that adjusted my dresses to fit my belly as it grew. It was a great idea. I had quite a few people tell me what an attractive pregnant lady I was. I had another great pregnancy.

One morning, I was painting my toenails, and my stomach started to hurt. I didn't think anything of it, but the pain continued. It didn't feel like the labor pains I had with Melissa. Thank God Ted was still home, and he said I might be getting ready to have the baby. He stuck his finger up my vagina and said he could feel the baby's head. He immediately called his OB (obstetric) friends from medical school and told them we were on our way to the hospital.

As we were leaving the house, I had to squat down from the pain, and I did a huge slimy poop right in the middle of the garage. Mark and Melissa thought it was funny but disgusting. I couldn't help it. We called a neighbor and left them next door.

My water broke all over Ted's car, and six minutes after I arrived at the hospital, I had Adam, our third child. Everyone there knew Ted from school, which I was thankful for. It was the worst pain I had ever been in, worse than labor. I had not planned on having a natural birth, and the nurse told me if I would quit screaming and use that energy to push, the baby would come out faster. She was right.

Out he came, all nine and a half pounds of him with a huge head. Thank God he was healthy. He was a meconium baby, meaning that he had a slight amount of his own stool (first type of feces passed by the baby was a dark greenish mass of desquamated cells, mucus, and bile that accumulated in the bowel of the fetus and was typically discharged shortly after birth) swallowed and breathed into his airway. The doctors were right on top of everything, and he was taken care of with no complications.

He was so big that I had to have an episiotomy, and they told me I might need to have surgery later. Thankfully, I didn't need to. He was actually raising his head up the next day, and I felt like I had just delivered a monster baby.

Now we had three children. Ted was doing his internship and decided to go into internal medicine. He said it was the most interesting to him because of the variety of diseases. Ted was very intelligent and he received five awards in medical school. I was so proud of him. He had gone through four years of medical school and one year of internship. Now he had to apply to different places to do his residency.

When I got home one day, he started singing "The Yellow Rose of Texas." I started screaming; we were going to Houston for his residency. Yahoo! We were going out West, to cowboy country. We didn't really want to be that far away from our families, but it would give us a chance to be in a totally different environment.

Ted's Residency

HOUSTON WAS TOTALLY AWESOME. WHAT THEY SAID about Texas was true; everything was bigger and better in Texas. The superhighways were very intimidating at first, with five or six overpasses everywhere you looked. They all drove like maniacs, and I had to go from one exit to the next just to get used to driving there. Eventually, I was a maniac driver like they were.

There were fabulous restaurants; three-story malls with ice-skating rinks in the middle of them; fantastic twenty-four-hour gyms with five floors, including an Olympic-size swimming pool and two spas; excellent public schools; and a hair-and-nail salon on every corner. I felt like we were definitely going to enjoy living here.

There was a gigantic church there that was so big that the Sunday school children's classes were divided by first initials of last names three at a time—for example, A–C, D–F, etc. The choir was like something out of Hollywood, and auditions were held before you could be in it.

A well-known makeup mogul had donated millions of dollars to the church, and it was beautiful inside with colorful stained glass in all the windows. Most of all, it was a church filled with the Holy Spirit. I was so happy I could take my children there. I felt I was getting closer and closer to God. My dad told me I didn't really grow up till I had kids. He was right.

Mark wanted to get baptized in the big baptismal tub full of water in front of the entire church. He was in the third grade, and I was so proud and happy that he wanted to do this. He wanted me to go with him, so we both got dunked and came up sopping wet. It was well worth the experience. All my kids had been baptized as babies, so this was something special.

I got the urge to have another baby. I already had three beautiful children, and everybody told me to be happy with the three I had. I was very happy with them, but for some reason, I still wanted another one. I asked God to take the desire away from me. I was forty-three years old, and I guess people thought I was high risk again.

I went to the church we had been attending and talked to a counselor there. I told her my situation, and she said the same thing everybody else did. She said, "Be happy with the three you have." I decided to just let God handle it and not be so concerned about it. Ted had been all for it. I would just continue my journey loving my family.

There was a picture of an angel on the wall at the counselor's office. She was a beautiful angel carrying a sweet little baby in her arms. I admired it, and the counselor said she had more prints, and she gave me one. I was so appreciative of her kindness.

I immediately took it to the nearest frame shop. The man who framed it for me was very open and easy to talk to. I told him my story about wanting to have a fourth baby and why the picture meant so much to me. I told him maybe I was too old to have a baby, even though two well-known and beautiful movie stars were pregnant at forty-three years old, my age. He told me not to let anything upset me. He had a heart attack awhile back, and he had learned that worry wasn't worth it. He said, "Do what gives you peace." He did a great job framing my picture, and I hung it on my bedroom wall. It gave me peace just to look at it.

A few weeks went by, and even though I continued going to the gym, I noticed my stomach was starting to stick out. I did a lot of abdominal exercises at the gym, so I noticed right away. I went to the doctor because I hadn't had my period on schedule. She did a pregnancy test on me, and I was nine weeks pregnant. I was so excited and so thankful to God. I was going to get my tubes tied earlier but was so glad I decided to wait.

I had actually been pregnant when I was talking to the counselor at the church. I had a connection with the picture of the angel carrying the baby in her arms. I felt like God was telling me that the angel was bringing me my baby. I just needed to be patient and wait for His timing.

Everyone told me how glowing I was when I was pregnant, and I had absolutely no complications. I did go to the gym but mostly swam in the Olympic-size pool. I swam a mile almost every day. Melissa was seven years old now and was so excited to be having a little sister. She had been putting up with two boys.

I had a very nice female obstetrician. She told me it would probably be best if I had a scheduled C-section. This would be my first scheduled one. With Mark, I was put under anesthesia; with Melissa, I had a quick block because she was stuck in my ribs; and I went natural with Adam. I wasn't sure what to expect.

I got into the delivery room, and Ted went with me. They proceeded to give me the epidural, and slowly, I lost all feeling from my waist down. I tried to move my legs, and I couldn't. I was starting to freak out. All of a sudden, I had a flashback of my internship in England when I worked with all the patients who were paraplegics and quadriplegics. I really thought I was losing it, but then Ted was so sweet and so supportive. He was right there beside me, telling me that everything was going to be fine, and held my hand the whole time. I felt such a deep bond with him then.

We finally had our fourth baby, and I had my tubes tied. That was it. Four was quite a job, but I was still thankful that God blessed me so. We named her Abigail. My surgical site was very painful, but they put me on a morphine drip. I was basically in la-la land.

While I was lying in the hospital bed, I noticed a sign on the wall next to my bed that warned the mother to be sure that the nurse who brought you your baby was the same nurse who took it to be weighed or whatever might be needed. Apparently, a baby had been stolen in a California hospital, and they had all the other hospitals on alerts. The nurse had just come in to take Abigail, my baby, to be weighed. Even though I was on the morphine drip and my surgical site was brand-new, I crawled out of bed holding my stomach with a pillow, brought the IV pole behind me, and crawled to the entrance of my door. I looked down the hall to be sure it was the same nurse with Abigail who had taken her. I sighed a sigh of relief that I could see both of them and waited till she came back into the room to get back into bed. The nurse was a bit alarmed when she saw me sitting on the floor beside my bed. I told her that the sign scared me, and she smiled and said she understood. She put Abigail back in her baby bed and helped me back into mine.

I thanked God again for Abigail and asked Him to please let me live long enough to watch her grow up. God is so awesome to always be there no matter what and always answers our prayers. I have learned that His ways and timing are not like my ways, but He knows the big picture, so we need to trust Him.

Ted's family and mine flew out to Houston for Abigail's christening. I was so happy to see my family, and it was nice that his family could make it also. I found a beautiful gown for Abigail, and we all had a big party afterward. Now I had four kids to take care of. I was so thankful that my dad had helped us out financially so I could stay home with them. Child care alone would have been expensive.

Mark was nine years old now and was still one of the biggest kids in his class. One day, he came home from school and told me another kid had called him a big fat tub of lard. It really hurt his feelings. He said he was going to beat him up. I told him not to touch him, and we would handle it differently.

I called his mom and told her what her son had said. She told me she would talk to him about it. She called me back and said that he told her he didn't say it. I told her that Mark wouldn't make up something like that, and her son was lying. When it came to my kids, my claws would come out; otherwise, I tried to get along with everyone. I told Mark not to do anything even though we knew he was wrong. Let's take the higher road.

The next day, I took him to the gym with me. He was in the fourth grade, and I got the biggest trainer there. He was tall, muscular, and very friendly. He worked with Mark every day for several months. Mark loved it. He would go after school and on weekends. He became very fit and healthy looking. No more "tub of lard" for him. The other kid was actually afraid of Mark then.

Melissa continued to be an easy child. She and I made friends with some sweet little girls and their moms. We did a lot of gymnastics and play days. There was so much to do in Houston that we were always busy. One of the moms, Katrina, gave me a huge baby shower, and her daughter, Kara, was Melissa's best friend. Both Melissa's and Mark's grades were good in school.

Adam was an easy child also. I guess compared to Mark, all three were much easier. I tried putting Adam in the mother's morning-out program of the church, but he didn't last long. He cried every time I took him, so I decided to just keep him home with Abigail and me.

I had to take Adam to the doctor one day because he had a bad cold and fever. Ted told me to just give him an over-the-counter fever/cold medicine. I got it and gave him the ordered amount. When we got home, I put the bottle up high in the counter in the kitchen so he couldn't reach it.

I put him down for a nap. He was not quite three now, and I thought he looked sleepy. I put Abigail down for a nap also and went back to check on Adam. He wasn't in his room where I left him, so I called for him. I searched the house and found him in the kitchen next to half a bottle of spilled medicine that I had just put up in the cupboard when we got back from seeing the doctor. I counted how many were left and realized that Adam had taken about half of the bottle of medicine.

He had put the stool up next to the counter and somehow gotten the medicine. I didn't even think about him doing that. I immediately called 911 and then called Ted. The ambulance came and didn't even turn on the siren. I never found out why not.

Adam was acting normal, but I knew the ER staff was going to have to do something quickly. Ted met us at the hospital. They made him drink a charcoal solution, and he didn't like it. They managed to get it down him with a feeding tube. I was so glad Ted was able to get away to meet us there.

He pooped out slimy black charcoal for about three days. I felt so badly about it and got cabinet and door locks after that. God and his angels saved us again. Little Adam could have overdosed and died. I would have never forgiven myself.

I felt so blessed to have four beautiful children, a loving and smart husband, and a great future ahead of us. I felt a deep sense of responsibility to be a good example for my kids, and I loved them so much.

Ted finally graduated from his residency program in internal medicine. We had thought about staying in Houston. We loved living there, and we had all made some nice friends. The only bad situation that I was happy to get away from was the drug problem. We lived near a very wealthy section of Houston where a lot of football players and celebrities lived. The high school students were dying from heroin overdoses, and it really scared me. One of my closest friends had a relative die from this satanic drug, and I thought about how horrible the drug world must be.

Ted decided we should move back to Florida so we could be closer to our families. I agreed with him. It would be nice to have our parents around as the kids got older, and I really felt like a Florida girl at heart.

Life in the Little City

WE ENDED UP IN A LITTLE CITY in Florida. It seemed so miniscule compared to Houston. Ted said he felt like we were in a third world because of the way people looked at the popular local mega shopping center. There definitely was a noticeable difference in the way people dressed and acted. Houston had so much more culture and sophistication.

Ted had gone ahead of me to an interview with the doctor he was interested in working with and at the same time found a house for us. I really should have gone with him, but I didn't want to have to take all four kids with us everywhere we went. The house was nice with two bedrooms upstairs and two downstairs. It was in a neighborhood with kids; and we got a trampoline, fort, sandbox, and swings like we had earlier. All the kids liked playing at our house. We were close to a lake, but we didn't live right on it, and there was a little wooded section behind us.

Ted's new office with an older doctor was in a small town nearby. He had kids Ted's age. Ted was now forty-two years old and starting out as a new doctor finally. It had been a long road of eight years of schooling after he had already gotten his BS in molecular cellular developmental biology. This was the class I never understood that my teacher's assistant had helped me get a C in.

The doctor whom Ted worked with lived on a private lake, and he and his wife invited us over for a barbecue. We rode around on their four-wheelers and had lots of fun. His wife was very sweet and was a psychologist. She had a face-lift and boob job and looked great. Two of their children were there, and we all got along well.

The kids liked to play in the neighborhood, which was small and gated, so I just told them to all stay together and watch out for one another. Back then it was safer than it is now. The other three were outside while Abigail and I stayed in the house. We were in the bathroom while I was putting on my makeup and using the curling iron. She was two years old then.

She kept pulling on my curling iron, and I was concerned that she might burn herself. I told her to go play in her room for a few minutes, and then I would play with her. After I was finished with my hair and makeup, I went to her room, and she wasn't there. I looked all over the house, yelling and calling her name. I started to get frantic when she didn't answer. I went outside and looked all over. I asked the other kids if they had seen her, and they said no.

Since we lived near a lake, I ran over to it to see if I could see anything. I couldn't find any evidence of her being there. Then I searched our backyard and still couldn't find her. My heart was sinking fast. I called 911 and told them I couldn't find my little girl. They said they were on their way.

I got down on my knees, cried, and prayed to God to keep Abigail safe and to help me find her alive and healthy. I frantically searched the house again and lifted up a blanket on the floor. There she was, all curled up, sleeping like a little angel. I thought of my picture of the angel holding the baby, which I had gotten from the church. I started crying with joy. God had saved us again. She could have wandered out of the house to the lake. I called the sheriff's office and told them I found her. I felt so guilty for not having more patience with her in the bathroom and not watching her more carefully.

I really hadn't met any of the other doctors' wives yet, but apparently, a lot of people already knew we were moving to town. One of the doctors' wives called me every day for two weeks just to chitchat. She gave me information on schools, shopping, and places of interest for the kids. We met for lunch and played tennis together when I could find a babysitter. She was very sweet and introduced me to her friends. Her husband, Rico, became good friends with Ted. Sanfra was pretty and very petite. I found out later that she was going through therapy because her husband was such a dog.

We were told that we should go to a private school because the public schools were not very good. I took all four of the kids with me, ranging in age from almost two years old to almost twelve years old, to visit the private school that was recommended to me. It was in a church at that time and seemed so small but quaint.

I walked into the office, which was attached to the church. There were three ladies in the office talking. I found out later that two of them were teachers, and the other was the secretary. It was still summertime, so school hadn't started yet. They had been expecting me and were very pleasant. We talked about the school for a while, and they told me to feel free to check the preschool out and look at the playground and campus. We had time to register if we liked it.

We looked around and liked what we saw; so I left Mark in charge of watching Melissa, Adam, and Abigail while I went back to talk about registration. As I entered the office, all the ladies' backs were turned, and they were gossiping about someone. I felt rather awkward, so I just stood there until they were finished. They were talking about a mother and her kids and how they were dressed and other ridiculous comments.

After listening a few more minutes, I realized that they were talking about me and my kids. I thought, *What unsophisticated women they were.* We had just moved from Houston. Did they expect us to look like them or even talk like them? I was furious.

I said, "Excuse me. I thought this was a Christian school." Since you find me and my children so different from you we probably won't fit in here after all. I think I'll try the public school down the road from where we live."

They turned around, and their mouths dropped. They were so embarrassed that they got caught gossiping about me. The looks on their faces were priceless. They tried to make up for it, but I was out of there.

The public school was nice, and everyone who worked there were very friendly. It would be more convenient for us because it was so close, and the private school was expensive. The only thing I didn't like about it was that the teacher/student ratio was too high for me. I liked the smaller classes that were offered at the private school.

The headmistress at the private school called me and apologized for the behavior of her employees and asked me to reconsider. She told me the ladies involved had been admonished. The secretary called me and told me she had tried to find my house so she could personally apologize.

I felt like I should forgive them because everybody gossiped a little bit. They just got caught. I certainly wasn't perfect, so I reconsidered and enrolled at Holy Shepherd School. I liked the name because I knew that we all need God's protection in our lives.

Thankfully, later, I found a beautiful boutique there that had clothes, shoes, jewelry, and purses that were just like the Houston clothes I wore and was similar to the boutiques I frequented while Ted was in medical school. The owner and I became good friends. The first day I went there, I had Abigail with me, and she was just a baby. I had on my gym clothes, and Tiffany, the owner, didn't know me. I was trying on clothes, and Abigail got my lipstick out of my purse and smeared it all over the carpet in the dressing room. I was horrified and didn't want to come out. I had to show Tiffany what happened, and she was so sweet about it. She said she would just get it cleaned and not to worry about it. I became one of her best customers after that, and everyone always compliments me when I have her clothes on. It is my eye candy fun place.

Mark entered the fifth grade, and Melissa entered the third grade. Mark actually had started to grow a beard now and looked much older than his age. I was praying that they would both make some good friends there. I kept Adam and Abigail home with me for a while till I knew more about the area's options.

Melissa's first best friend was a doctor's kid. They spent all their time together. I met her mom also, and we became friends. Later, Melissa became friends with a boy whose mom was very nice. I related to her more because she actually dressed nicer than most of the other moms. His father was a lawyer, and our families became good friends because Mark was friends with their older son.

There was a lot of money around in citrus and land because grandpas passed it down to their sons who passed it down to their sons. I loved seeing all the orange groves everywhere, and as time passed, it made me sad to see them torn down to build housing complexes. The aroma of the orange blossoms reminded me of my childhood. My dad had several orange groves, and it was fun to pick our own oranges.

Mark made friends with everyone he met. He had my social, friendly personality and soon became the BMOC at school. He not only looked older but he also acted older and ended up being the bodyguard of the lawyer's kid. I only knew this because his mother told me. Apparently, this kid had a heart condition, and Mark wanted to keep him away from bullies.

One of Mark's friends was a kid whose father used to be a professional baseball player when he was younger. His name was Doug. Mark spent the night with Doug for a sleepover, and they were watching a movie on television. They decided to make a crank call to their music teacher, who definitely was not one of their favorite teachers at school.

The movie was playing in the background while they made the call, and there were a bunch of cuss words being said while they were on the phone. She assumed the boys said them, and she had caller ID. The next morning, I get a phone call from the headmistress, and she wanted me to come to her office. When I got there, Mark, Doug, and his dad were sitting there with Mrs. Starr, the headmistress. The music teacher was also there.

The music teacher, Mrs. Viola, accused the boys of shouting obscenities to her over the phone. They told her it was the movie in the background and not them. She didn't believe them. The headmistress said she was going to expel the boys even though they apologized.

I told her, if she expelled them, I was going to call my attorney, our friend whose boys knew Mark and Melissa, and call the local newspaper and tell them all the gossip I knew about some of the employees at the school.

One of the administrators had been involved with a prostitute, and I knew they didn't want that leaked to the public. It would look bad for the school's image. The boys were not expelled, and Doug's father gave me a high five and said he was proud of me for having so much moxie. I told him my claws always come out when I need to protect my kids. Later, I found out that Doug died from a heroin overdose when he was in his twenties. It makes me so sad.

Mark also told me, when he entered middle school, that drugs were big on campus. Since Mark always had looked older than his age, he had made friends with some of the older students there. He told me some of the seniors asked him if he wanted some pot. I was very upset about this, but Mark, of course, wouldn't tell me who they were. I was glad that he at least made me aware of it.

The longer we lived in Water City, the more I realized what a gossipy little redneck town it was. The only good thing about it was all the beautiful lakes there, hence its name.

The kids did well in school, and Melissa and Abigail liked dance and soccer. I liked most of the moms, but there were a few really snobby women there. They had no reason to be either. Several of my friends told me I was one of the few women they liked there because there were so many snobs. My mom had called me a reverse snob when I was in high school because I couldn't stand snobby people even back then. Thankfully, I did manage to get along with most of the women there, and I knew they were getting a good education for the most part.

When Adam was in the fifth grade, the headmistress voted him the most likely to succeed. I was so proud of him. He had some nice friends and played soccer on the city team. He was the star player. Ted didn't come to many of the games, but he did come occasionally.

Mark played basketball on the city league, and Ted helped coach. He almost got into a fistfight with one of the other coaches Mark's team was playing against. This coach was also a doctor. Doctors' egos get in the way a lot. Mark had wanted to play on the school basketball team, but they gave away scholarships to kids who "just happened" to be great basketball players. When I questioned the headmaster about it, he lied to my face and said that wasn't true. I lost all respect for him. The school continued to do it the whole time we were there.

Life was good and I was happy staying home with the kids, being a taxi driver, and hosting sleepovers. I was so thankful I didn't have to work and leave them all day. Nurses' hours made it difficult to juggle taking care of the kids and working.

We found a church we liked and went as a family just about every Sunday. The kids would go to Sunday school. The stained glass at the front of the church was and still is the most beautiful stained glass I have ever seen, even better than what the old European churches had. It is a full-length window of Jesus standing with his arms open, waiting for you to come to Him. I would go in there and pray during the week, with the sanctuary all to myself, and just admire and feel comforted praying while I looked at Jesus' face.

Meanwhile, Ted started working for a different doctor in Water City. The doctor was also older, but he was a little strange. He was very well-liked, though, in the community. He had a second younger wife, who was also a doctor in a city nearby. She was very money hungry and pretentious. They invited us to their house, and it was very grandiose. She had the biggest walk-in closet I have ever seen. It was as big as a medium-sized bedroom. All four walls were covered with racks of clothes, shoes, and handbags from the high ceilings to the carpeted floor. She had a push-button system that would rotate the racks down one at a time so she could reach them. I was flabbergasted.

She was committing Medicare fraud as a dermatologist. She was taking multiple biopsies off people who really didn't need it. She told me she just wanted to be sure she didn't overlook anything. I believed her, especially since they weren't going to take off my second melanoma when Ted was in medical school if we hadn't insisted.

She finally ended up being investigated by the FBI. They went to her office with guns and arrested her. Her fancy attorneys couldn't keep her from serving a jail sentence. I felt sorry for her husband. He was a really nice guy. We had planned on going to a Fourth of July party with him, but he had a heart attack and died that day. Ted said it was probably because of all the stress his wife had put him through.

Now Ted was the only doctor in the office, and he bought the practice and the building. It was a nice little office in a good location. We remodeled it, and he was happy with his job. He kept all the patients who had been seeing the other doctor, as well as his own. He was very busy and thankfully had a good and faithful nurse there to help him, and she was a Christian. The office staff was very helpful in making changes that were needed.

Mark decided he wanted to go to public school for high school. I wanted him to stay at Holy Shepherd, but he kept insisting, so we said yes, as long as his grades were good. He told me there were drugs at both schools. This really concerned me, but all I could do was pray. I was so naive that I didn't even think about anything except pot being a problem there.

I was unaware of the fact that Mark was smoking pot at that time. I knew some of the kids at Holy Shepherd were smoking and even some of the parents. I thought he was too young to be doing that in high school, but I remembered that, years ago, some of the kids in my high school were smoking pot. I was just afraid to at that time.

Ted and I were going to Holy Shepherd for one of the girls' performances, and Ted pulled out a joint and asked me if I wanted to smoke it with him. I was so surprised. I really didn't know what to say or do. I hadn't smoked since a year before we had Mark. I smoked it with him but wished I hadn't. We went to the performance, and I felt very weird, like I was in another dimension. I started wondering about what might be going on and why Ted had the joint in the first place. I also felt like a hypocrite to my kids.

The Beginning of the Drug World

MARK AND TED WERE BOTH GOING TO the gym on a regular basis. I went in the mornings, and they went in the evenings when Ted got off work. I noticed that both of them were getting noticeably more muscular and would compare their muscles with each other to see whose were bigger. I was getting kind of sick of listening to them.

I was cleaning Mark's bathroom while he was at school, and I found a bottle of steroids in one of his drawers. I wasn't sure what it was at first, so I kept it and showed it to Ted. He confirmed that it was steroids and told me that he and Mark were both taking them. He said Mark was injecting them, and he was taking them orally. I was so angry at both of them. To begin with, they didn't need to take steroids, and there were many side effects. One of the side effects was their balls shrinking and mood swings. I found it rather ironic that they were taking the steroids to make them look manlier with bigger muscles and then not having balls because of it.

Ted said he knew what they were doing and how to take them correctly. He reminded me that he had majored in molecular cellular developmental biology and that he was a doctor. I didn't give a poop and told him it was wrong, and he was being a bad example for his son. Ted gained forty pounds and had a huge neck and arms. I liked him better when he was just the way he was when I met him. Mark gained thirty pounds. I told Mark I didn't want him taking them, and he said Dad said it was okay. They were both turning into the kind of men I couldn't stand at the gym. They were always looking at themselves in the mirror and flexing. I told Mark that going to the gym was supposed to help keep you healthy, not put something potentially dangerous into your body. He didn't care about what I said. There was nothing I could do but pray.

Ted started to get so busy that he was getting overwhelmed and decided he would hire a nurse practitioner. He ended up hiring a woman I had met at an eye clinic where she worked. She had told me that her kids went to Holy Shepherd and that it was a good school. She seemed to be nice and friendly. He now had a full staff. My favorites were his two nurses and the office manager.

We decided to put Adam in another Christian school that was smaller but also had a good reputation. Adam made some good friends there and played on the basketball team. He was the biggest kid there and would just stand under the basket and wait for his team members to throw him the ball so he could dunk it.

Adam was the BMOC at the new school. He was tall with blonde hair and blue eyes. He looked more like Ted than Mark did. Someone accused Adam and one of his friends of meeting in the bathroom and exchanging little baggies of pot. No one accused him of smoking it, and nothing was ever proven. I felt like some of the other kids were jealous of him and were trying to get him in trouble. In fact, I felt like people were jealous of our whole family.

My friends were always telling me what a beautiful family I had. We had a very good photographer in town take a family picture of us outside on a dock by a lake. It was a gorgeous picture. Ted put one up in his office, and the patients were always complimenting him on it. I put the other one up in our house. The only weird thing about the photography session was that Ted kept talking about women posing naked in a popular magazine to the photographer. Finally, the photographer told him that he had a beautiful wife and that he shouldn't be talking that way. I immediately gained more respect for the photographer and had him take family pictures later.

I decided to work two nights a week at an Alzheimer's unit near our house just to keep my nursing skills up to date. I worked nights so I could take the kids to school, and Ted was there to watch them while I worked. I had kept my nursing license active and couldn't believe that some of my nurse friends let their license expire without renewing it. I told them not to completely rely on their husbands for income. Anything could happen.

One of the nurse's aides I worked with was quite a rough character, but I really liked her. She had actually killed somebody in self-defense and had gone after her ex-husband with a power saw. One night, we heard some helicopters circling over our workplace and wondered what was going on. We called the police to find out, and they told us there was an escapee in our area. I was very upset about it, but Maggie, my nurse's aide friend, said not to worry and that she would protect me, and I believed her. Thankfully, the police called us back and said they caught him.

I would pick up Adam or go to his basketball games after working all night. I already had dry, sensitive eyes and had to put eye drops in them. When I worked nights, they would get even redder, and it was very tiring working nights.

The women at the school started a rumor about me that I was smoking pot, and that was why my eyes were so red. I was really ticked off when I found out about it and went straight to the principal. I told him while I was working all night, taking care of Alzheimer's patients, these gossipy women were sleeping. They had already been talking about Adam, and I didn't appreciate it. I told him I thought this was supposed to be a Christian school and that they were wrong about their assumptions.

He was very nice about it and said that he was sorry it happened and that they shouldn't have been gossiping. He also said that just because they were Christians, it didn't mean they were perfect, just forgiven. He was right. The same gossiping had happened at Holy Shepherd, and I think they were just jealous. I forgave them and moved on but learned to be very careful whom I trusted in this little town. I felt sorry for them that they had nothing better to do.

I decided to quit work because the girls were getting older. Abigail was playing a lot of soccer, and I would take her and some of the girls on the team to away games. Melissa's passion was dance. She took lessons at the local dance studio and danced at school. My days were still happy being a chauffeur.

While the kids were all in school, I had some spider veins treated on my legs by one of Ted's nursing assistants. While she was doing the procedure, she noticed a mole on my lower leg. She showed it to Ted, and it ended up being my third melanoma. I had it taken off, and again, it was a level 1. God saved me again. There were many people who died from melanomas. I thanked Eve, Ted's nursing assistant, for being so observant and helping save my life. I felt like He kept saving me for a reason as He did for everyone. If you are still alive, it is because God wants you to be.

We decided that, since Ted was making more money now, it would be nice to live on one of the beautiful lakes in Water City. After all, that was how the city got named. I started looking at houses, and after checking out several that I didn't like, I found the perfect house for us.

The minute I walked through the front door, I knew Ted would love the house. It was on two acres, and it was on the point of two different lakes connected by a short canal. It had a nice pool and dock, and I knew this was the perfect house for our family. I couldn't wait to tell Ted about it.

He loved it also. We had to sell our house quickly. Ted and the owner of the house we wanted went back and forth on the price for several months. They finally compromised. We put a down payment on it, and thankfully, ours sold right away. We were so excited to be living on the water. It was our dream house.

Unfortunately, the new owners of our old house experienced a sinkhole soon after we moved out. They tried to sue us but lost. There was no way for us to know that was going to happen. I felt bad about it, but at the same time, I was glad it didn't happen when we were there.

We put more money into house remodeling. We got rid of the carpet and put in wooden floors. We remodeled the kitchen and two of the bathrooms. We also found a very good interior designer to help us make the house more beautiful. We were very pleased with the results.

Ted bought a nice, expensive boat and a jet ski. We all had so much fun skiing, wakeboarding, and tubing. We were living the life, and I was so happy and thankful to God. We had big birthday parties for Abigail with slip and slides, inflatable gyms and slides, and bounce houses. We also had a trampoline and a swing set. The hammock was fun too.

We always had kids of all ages over, and the house was never quiet. We had a nice older couple on one side of us and another nice couple a little older than us on the other. The sunsets were absolutely gorgeous overlooking the lake, and I felt like I was in heaven.

We all went on a trip to San Francisco because Ted had a meeting there. It was fun to see the Golden Gate Bridge and walk across it. We went to Fisherman's Wharf, Alcatraz Island, and Chinatown and rode the cable cars. It was so nice to get away and do something as a family without any work concerns.

We went on another vacation later to Alaska. That was even more fun because it was so different from anything we had done before. We took a cruise ship from Seattle, and the kids had a blast with the ship's activities. We flew in a helicopter to a glacier and rode dogsleds through the snow. It was like we were in a movie. We shopped and bought some of their famous jewelry made from gold quartz. Ted and I were having fun together again, and it was a good feeling.

The only bad situation we had on the trip was when Mark and Ted almost got in a fistfight with some guy on the ship. He had saved ten seats on the front row of the theater. We were all looking forward to seeing the show and got there early so we could get good seats. When we sat down in the empty seats on the front row, this fat guy said they were already saved. He became rather belligerent until Ted and Mark stood up in front of him, and he then decided he didn't want to cause a problem. We stayed where we were and enjoyed the show.

As the kids got older, the parties started to change. Mark had a huge party one night when he was in high school. Since he had started going to public school, I didn't know all his friends like I did in private school. That had been another good thing about private school. It was easier to find out about a kid and his family if you really wanted to.

The party was in the back room closest to the lake. We had a sliding glass door back there, so I knew they were coming in and out of the house. The music was loud, and I noticed they were drinking a lot of water. I thought it was because they were sweaty from dancing.

Ted came out of the room and told me he and Mark had just "tried" some ecstasy. I really didn't know much about drugs except pot, but I had heard about kids doing ecstasy, and I knew it was illegal. It was called a "designer drug," and kids were dying from using it. I totally freaked out and asked him why he would do that. He said he was just curious.

I was furious. Those kids were doing ecstasy in my house, and I needed to get them out of there before our neighbors called the cops. It ticked me off even more when Ted went to his room and went to sleep. I wondered what was going on with him. First, he was doing steroids and now ecstasy. He was turning into someone I didn't like to be my children's father.

I had told Mark before the party that I wanted everyone gone by 1:00 a.m. I checked the back room to make sure everyone was gone when they were supposed to. The back room was empty, but I heard noises from outside the house. I went outside and there was a big group of teenagers partying in our driveway. I looked for Mark in the crowd, but none of the kids knew where he was.

I checked his room, and he was sound asleep. I told him his so-called friends were partying without him in our driveway. He was just as angry as I was, got up, and told everybody to get out of our yard. He told me he had told them to leave before he went to bed. We didn't have any more parties like that again.

I talked to Mark about the ecstasy and told him I didn't want him doing any more drugs. I was at my wit's end, and I felt like I was going crazy. I couldn't believe that Ted would do ecstasy at his own son's party. It made me sick.

We had a friend who had big Halloween parties that we loved to go to. They lived across the lake from us. She would decorate her house for three days, getting ready for the party. It looked like a professional decorator had helped her. Everyone would dress up with lots of tits and ass showing, and the liquor was flowing. I had learned by now that I wasn't a good drinker, and I had the kids to think about.

After one of the parties, I found out from a friend of mine that her husband had asked Ted where I was. His reply was that I was probably upstairs screwing somebody. In actuality, I was outside talking to the babysitter to make sure everything was going smoothly. Her husband was a nice Christian guy, and he was just as upset by what Ted said as I was. I just couldn't understand why Ted would say something like that. I knew he was probably drinking too much.

There was a professional photographer at the party to take our pictures. I thought Ted and I looked great. He was a gladiator, and I was a French maid. Everybody told me how sexy I looked. Ted never complimented me anymore.

Mark continued to be my biggest challenge as far as the kids went. I think a lot was going on behind my back with him and Ted and drugs. I was just not sure when it all started after the steroids and ecstasy. Mark got a new girlfriend when he was seventeen years old, and she was nineteen. He would go over to her house at five thirty in the morning before school. I talked to her mother about it, and she said they were fine and that she was watching them while they watched television. I thought it was all a bunch of crap, and I told her so.

She told Mark that she couldn't get pregnant and then surprisingly ended up pregnant with Mark's kid. I had told Mark while he was dating her that she was lying and that I would disinherit him if he got her pregnant. I was hoping this would scare him into at least wearing some protection.

She got an abortion. Mark was so distraught and cried and cried for days. He said he had wanted to keep the baby. I was very concerned about him and didn't want him to do something stupid. I was also hoping that what I had said didn't influence Latrice, his girlfriend, into getting the abortion. I had felt like maybe she was somewhat of a gold digger. I cried also over the whole situation.

Mark had a good friend in high school named Charlie. He was the kind of kid that everyone liked. He was a great swimmer and on the swim team at high school. He lived across the lake from us.

One night, Charlie and another kid, Rhett, were at his house. Rhett's father was a wealthy landowner, who, of course, inherited land from his father. Two black guys knocked on the door and demanded to come in. Apparently, Rhett owed them some money for drugs. He had told them that he didn't have the money, but his friend Charlie did. One thing led to another, and Charlie was shot in the arm by one of the black guys, who panicked and ran. Rhett called his father, who called his attorney. They did not call 911 until the attorney got the story straight. Charlie was bleeding the whole time, but I guess Rhett's dad cared more about protecting his son than he did about Charlie's life. Charlie died in the ambulance on the way to the hospital.

The two families were friends before that, but there was a huge lawsuit over the situation, which there should have been. There were so many people at Charlie's funeral that people were standing in the back. Rhett ended up moving to California and trying to be a rapper. How could he or his father live with themselves knowing what they had done? Just because Rhett's dad had megabucks, somehow, they got away with it. They were good friends with the sheriff.

The sheriff and his redneck cops were pretty shifty. The sheriff, Randy Sands, thought he was God. He even went around to the churches in town and gave speeches in his uniform. When he came to my church, I didn't go. He was always acting like he was such a great man, but a lot of people didn't like him. Most of the cops were control freaks and were probably nerds in high school, at least that was what one of Mark's girlfriends said, who was a dispatcher. I did meet a few nice cops, though, but very few.

Rhett's father had a brother-in-law who was quite a flirt around town. He was also in business with the selfish, snobby, wealthy redneck family. In fact, Rhett's older brother told Mark that his family owned Water City. That made me feel sorry for the little brat, but in a way, there was some truth to that. The brother-in-law had a trunk load of cocaine in his car. That night, he died of a heart attack. A cocaine overdose has a massive effect on the heart.

If it had been anyone else in town who had been found dead at their house and a trunk load of cocaine was discovered, it would have been all over the front page of the local newspaper. Not one word was mentioned about the cocaine, just that he died of a heart attack. That's how crooked the sheriff and his posse are in our little town. I give them some credit, though. They have busted some big meth operations and prostitution stings.

By now, I started to realize that Mark was heavy in drugs, but I didn't know exactly what or how often. I had a horrible feeling that Ted was doing them with him, but I had no proof. I was putting some clean shirts in Ted's closet when I noticed something sticking out of one of his coat pockets. There were ten $100 bills neatly folded in his pocket I wondered why he would have that much money just stashed in his pocket.

I asked him about it, and he said that he kept it there so Mark wouldn't sell drugs for money like he did when he was in college. At first, I believed him until one of Mark's girlfriends, Lisa, told me that she did heroin with Mark and Ted in our bathroom. I didn't know if she was telling the truth or not. I was so unhappy and starting to get depressed about the whole drug world scene. I cried and cried and asked God to help us all. Later that week, Mark and Lisa were at a local hotel, and the people next to them called the cops because they heard Mark and Lisa arguing. Mark called me, and when I got to the hotel, the cops were there, searching the room. They found some syringes, and they all tested negative for any drugs. They were all clean. After the cops left, Mark told me he didn't know how the syringes tested clean because they had been shooting up heroin right before the cops arrived. Only by a miracle could those syringes have tested negative. Even Mark agreed with me, and I told Lisa to leave, and Mark came home with me. Now I was starting to believe that Lisa was telling the truth about Mark, Ted, and her doing the heroin together.

Several weeks later, Ted told me there was more of the Mafia in him than I realized. He told me he had Lisa beat up and left on the side of the road. I thought he was joking at first, but he was actually telling the truth and showed absolutely no remorse. I was starting to lose my respect for him and wondering who he was. He wasn't the man I married anymore.

Mark's grades had always been very good, but they were starting to slip. I couldn't understand what was going on except I knew it wasn't anything good. One night, Mark called me and said he had been pulled over by the cops. He told me where he was and to come quickly. As soon as I got there, he told me he had just dropped off his friend Kline, who lived right down the street. The two cops lied to me and told me they were doing a random pullover. They searched Mark's truck and found heroin in it. I didn't even know what heroin looked like. I flashed back to Houston where all those high school students were dying from heroin overdoses. The cops kept asking Mark where he got it from so he would get an easier sentence. He and I both said that we were going to call our attorney. It was obvious that the kid he had just dropped off had ratted on Mark to save his own butt. Mark didn't want to say who he got it from, and the cops were so pissed off.

I had anointed the driver's mirror and the passenger mirror on Mark's truck a few days before with anointing oil, asking God to protect Mark. A very devoted Christian friend of mine had introduced me to the power of anointing oil with prayer. I put anointing oil all over my house, asking God to protect my family.

I was a nervous wreck. I could not even fathom the thought that I would ever have a son who was doing heroin. That happened to other lowlife people, not to people like me. Unfortunately, Satan strikes at everyone.

I wondered how the heroin use even got started. Mark had a friend, Woody, who always went to the bathroom every time he came over. I asked Mark about it, and he said he had some kind of bowel problem. He was very thin and pale, so I believed him. This kid was so smart that he made the highest score ever on an engineering preadmission test to an Ivy League school in the East. I thought, *Great, he will be a good example for Mark to make better grades like he used to.*

Later, Mark told me he had been doing heroin with this kid. I was so disgusted and then started to feel sorry for him because Mark told me that both of Woody's parents did heroin, and so did his sister. This kid and his sister had horrible examples for parents. Who knew what their parents were like? It made me very angry just to think about what a great life Woody could have had and how much he could contribute to society if he was straight. If you can't be good examples for your children, then don't have them. That was pure child abuse. That was why it makes me so angry when the cops want to just throw them in jail. There is a program in Massachusetts where the police actually provide treatment for drug users. Isn't that the right thing to do? What a kind person to think of that program. Hopefully, programs like this will spread everywhere.

Our attorney, Calvin, told me they wanted to put Mark in jail for the night, and then he would go see him in the morning. We had known Calvin and his family ever since we moved from Houston. Mark got bailed out the next morning.

Since Mark was still a minor and Calvin was such a great attorney, Mark didn't have to stay in jail. He got to go to an alternative adult school, finish his high school diploma, and do some community hours. I made him get his graduation picture with his cap and gown.

I didn't realize he was still doing heroin in adult school. He was so smart that he still made good grades. I was so naive that I didn't realize it till Ted said something about not liking Mark's graduation picture because he knew he was on heroin then. I couldn't believe he said that. Why didn't he do something about it then? Was he doing the heroin with him? Was Mark buying the heroin for both of them with the money that was in Ted's coat pocket? I thought so, but nobody would confess to me.

After he got his diploma, it became obvious even to me that he needed help. He ended up in the lockdown unit at the local hospital for detox. I was so sad to see him in there, but I prayed that he would get some help from the professionals.

After his stay at the hospital, our attorney got him into a Christian rehab, which was two hours away. He relapsed by taking an antidepressant, and they thankfully sent him to another location of the same rehab further north about eight hours away. I thanked them and God for giving him another chance. He ended up being there for sixteen months. I would visit him every month by myself, except once when Ted went with me. I had made friends with some of the guys at the rehab, and they told me they could tell that Ted was a drug abuser. I asked them how they could tell, and they said just by looking at him. I never understood that. I found out later that Mark had told some of his friends that his dad would probably be bringing some drugs with him when he came. That proved what the guys said about him was true.

The whole family went to see Mark when he finally graduated. He was humble and acted the way he had before he was doing drugs. I was so happy to have my healthy son back. Lisa, the girlfriend whom Ted had beaten up, was spreading a rumor that Mark had tried to hang himself at the rehab. I had been frantic till I heard his voice. I wanted her to know that Mark was home, and she was never allowed in our house again.

Ted was like a different person from the man I married. He was like Dr. Jekyll and Mr. Hyde. He had always been arrogant and somewhat vain; but now he was narcissistic, arrogant, and extremely moody. He had a hair transplant and wore his hair down on his forehead while it was growing out. One of my friends asked me if he was going for a new look because he always had beautiful wavy blonde hair. Once it all grew out again, he grew it long, and his patients called him Surfer Boy. He bought a beautiful $160,000 Bentley and started making more money than ever. Unfortunately, he forgot who God was.

His mother, Nita, moved to Water City and found a little house down the street from us. Ted kept remarking about how unhappy she was living with Anthony because he kept drinking. I told Ted to have her move near us but not to let Anthony know where she was. She promised she wouldn't. One month later, Anthony was living with her. They had that codependent relationship that couldn't be broken. I felt sorry for both of them until Ted stopped going to church with us and started going to the Catholic church with his mother. I felt like he was favoring his mother over his family. She could have come with us, or he could have gone with her every once in a while. I was not happy with the situation.

Some of my friends told me that they had seen Ted and his nurse practitioner, Isabel, at the gym together. I didn't think much of it because I knew they both worked out. She had told me that both her parents were three hundred pounds, and she never wanted to get that way. She did have a good body, but her face was very rough looking. She didn't seem a threat to me at that time.

Water City was such a Podunk full of gossipers. There was a rumor going around town that Isabel's daughter was really Ted's. Well, to begin with, we were still living in Houston six years after Isabel's daughter was born, and she looked exactly like her dad. I told my friend who told me the rumor that Ted would have had the longest penis in history to be her father. That was definitely not true, and I thought, *What idiot would start that rumor?*

Then I had another girlfriend tell me that Isabel was following Ted everywhere he went at a party at a friend's house. It was a jet ski and boat party in the middle of the day, and I didn't get out in the sun because of my melanomas. Also, the younger kids would have been too much to look after at a pool party full of drunks. Now I started thinking that maybe there was some truth to these rumors I had been told.

The Realization of the Big Betrayal

I WAS AT A BIG PARTY AT one of my friends' house, and we were all talking about boats and tubing our kids in the lakes. That was when one of my other friends told me she had seen Ted and Isabel at the boat dock, getting ready to take Isabel's boat out with just the two of them. She said she wasn't going to mention it to me, but since I was there at the party, she said she thought I would want to know. Isabel was wearing a string bikini. I thought it was kind of odd that she would mention that, but I guess she was trying to make a point.

I couldn't really explain how hurt I was. How could he cheat on me after all we had gone through together? I was there through medical school, internship, residency, and four kids. I made his lunch every day and always put a little note in his lunch box, letting him know I was thinking of him. I tried to make them funny or romantic and let him know I loved him. When I thought about the fact that he was going to work every day and she was there, it tore me up inside.

When I confronted him about my friend seeing him and Isabel at the boat dock, he said that her husband was out of town, so he helped her with the boat. I knew it was a lie, but I just kept my mouth shut, knowing it would cause a fight if I pursued it further.

I didn't trust him at all now, and my respect for him was gone also. I decided to stay for the kids' sake, mainly because the thought of my kids possibly being with Isabel was too much for me to bear. Ted said some weird things to me. He said he and Isabel were talking that if they got together, since they both worked, who would take care of the kids? He also asked me if I would want to get a separation for two years and then get back together again because we would probably miss each other. He was crazy and out of his mind, and I told him so. I just had to learn to live with him, but I never could have done it without God's help. He kept me sane and stable to be able to take care of the other kids.

I knew that some of my other girlfriends' husbands were cheating on them, and they stayed together for the kids and the money. I just never thought it would happen to me. It was so sad to think of how infidelity affected so many people's lives.

Mark was in and out of detox/rehabs several times. I thought he was going to be okay after the first one, but he went right back into his drug relapse about six months after he got home. One rehab said hot saunas and mega doses of niacin would help. It didn't. Another said the problem was mold. I had all my air-conditioning vents cleaned and had the best filters put in with ultraviolet lights, which were supposed to cut down on mold. Mark did say he felt like the air was cleaner. The last rehab he went to helped him, and he admitted that he should have stayed longer but left early. Altogether, we spent more than $60,000 on drug programs for him.

Each time I would go to visit him at the rehabs, I would be hopeful that this one would be the last one and that he would stay straight. Then I finally got it. The person who is doing drugs has to "want" to quit badly enough to actually quit. I don't believe it is a disease, like so many of the rehabs claimed. You can be influenced by others, especially in your own family, but God is stronger than anything Satan can do. I told Mark to put God first and rely on Him. He listened to me but not enough to change his ways. I continued to pray for him and ask for God's favor and protection. He helped me cope with situations I had no control over, or I would have lost my mind.

Somehow, by the grace of God, Mark managed to finish two years of junior college at the local school. He made good grades in spite of whatever he was on at that time. I never knew for sure. He wrecked his car and should have died. Then he bought a motorcycle, wrecked it also, and was saved again. I told him he was like a cat with nine lives, and his guardian angels were working overtime with him.

I then started having issues with Adam. He had always been a straight A student, and his grades started slipping once he hit public high school. I put him back into Holy Shepherd, the private school, because I felt like the smaller school had more structure. Mark had told me there were drugs there, but I still wanted to try it again. Abigail was still there. Adam met a girl at the school who asked him if he wanted to go smoke some pot in the parking lot. She had it with her. He said yes, and one of the other students—a fat, little rich kid—saw them and told the administration. I got called for a meeting with Adam and the administrators, and they decided to expel Adam and the other two students involved. I told them that there were many kids who smoked pot there, and I also knew of some parents. Adam was just influenced by the girl and made a bad choice. I told one of the administrators that what went around came around. He said he didn't know what I was talking about. I knew his kid was in a band, and pot was an issue there. His kid got arrested for smoking pot not long after Adam got expelled.

In all fairness, though, they did say if Adam wanted to come back later, he could if his grades were good. They also did not call the cops, and the sheriff liked to put kids in jail. I wondered what the sheriff was like when he was in high school. Adam said he wanted to stay at the public high school because he was on the football team and was one of the best players. He was 6'4" and 220 pounds by then.

I started getting phone calls from Adam's counselor that Adam was skipping school a lot. She was a friend of mine and said she was concerned about him. She said if he really wanted to get a football scholarship, his grades would need to improve. I talked to him about it, and he said he would do better.

He met a girl, Tessa, whom he really liked. I liked her when I first met her. Adam and Tessa went to a party and were drinking with the rest of the teenagers, but Adam also took some anti anxiety pills. He was driving his truck to leave the party and hit a tree. He did $6,000 worth of damage to his truck. I was so ticked off and sold his truck. I started driving him to school and picking him up to make sure he got to school and stayed there; so I thought.

He still managed to skip school. I actually caught him walking to a friend's house during school as I was on my way to run an errand. He was with another kid, and a cop had stopped them. The other kid's mother was already there. Both of us moms were really upset. The cop was nice and told us to just take them home. I was so thankful. I told

Adam I couldn't handle much more. Ted was in another world by now and didn't help me discipline at all.

Adam didn't have a truck, but he and Tessa managed to get together somehow. Apparently, they had sex; and when Tessa's alcoholic mother found out about it, she threatened to have Adam arrested for rape. Thank God Tessa's best friend told her that Tessa was not a virgin when she met Adam. Tessa finally confessed, and her mother backed off. I wanted Adam to just stay away from her and Tessa's crazy mother.

Tessa's alcoholic mother told me she always watched Adam and Tessa when he was over there. At 3:00 a.m., Adam still wasn't home. I drove over to Tessa's house and was pounding on the door, and their dog started barking. Finally, the mom came to the door, looking hung over, and I went in and found Adam and Tessa sleeping in her bed. I was furious and told her mother what a great job she did of watching them. I told Adam he could either come home with me or find another place to live. He came home with me. I was so sad and unhappy.

He promised me he would stay in school if I would get him some transportation. Ted and I got him another truck, and I told him if he skipped school again, the truck would go. He also had to bring up his grades as part of the deal.

Ted started acting even more distant. I begged him to stop his affair with Isabel, the jezebel, and get another nurse practitioner. He said she made us a lot of money. I told him I didn't care. We could sell the house and get a less expensive one or even move out of town. I asked him to put his hand on the Bible and tell me he wasn't sleeping with Isabel. He did, but I knew he was lying.

One day, I couldn't stand it any longer. I went to his office and walked in to Isabel's side of the office. Our beautiful family picture was on display there at the entrance for all the patients to see. When I got to her office, she was just sitting there, and I asked her if I could talk to her. She was very nice at first and actually let me hold her hands and pray together. She told me she had lost her faith when her sister died. Her sister's husband had shot her sister and killed her. Isabel said she felt like she could have stopped him, but I tried to tell her it wasn't her fault.

Then Ted came in and started calling me a psycho freak right in front of all the patients. Then Isabel started calling me a psycho also. She had told me it wasn't all her fault, that it takes two. I was so embarrassed that I just ran out of the building.

There were two nurses who worked closely with Ted. One of them, Sunny, told me point-blank that Ted and Isabel had been having an affair for quite a while. She didn't want to get involved at first but said that she felt like I should know. She told me that Isabel's husband was suspicious also.

Isabel's husband, John, called me up one day, and we talked in his car while we went for a ride. He said he knew Ted and Isabel were seeing each other. They had also been e-mailing each other. Isabel had actually brought the computer into the office so John couldn't have access to it. John tried to blame it mostly on Ted, and I told him that one of Ted's nurses had already told me that Isabel was literally throwing herself at him. I also told him that my friends knew about it also. Either way, it was wrong, and I was starting to get depressed about it.

After Ted bought his Bentley, Isabel bought another less expensive sports car like his previous one and a golden retriever like ours and named it Boomer, like ours. I thought that was pretty weird.

She tried to get friendly with Mark and Melissa and actually started jogging with Mark. When I found out about it, I told him I would throw him out of the house if he continued to jog with her. Then I started getting suspicious that one of the bonds that Ted and Isabel had was that they were doing drugs together and possibly with Mark. I didn't know what to think anymore.

Isabel already had a reputation around town as being a jezebel. It was rumored that she was sleeping with another doctor in town who she jogged with. He was a friend of Ted's. He told me that Ted had taken away his jogging partner. That irritated me. It was also rumored that she was sleeping with one of her neighbors, a black principal of a local school. He was trying to flirt with me one day at the gym and asked my name. I told him and said I was married to Ted. His mouth dropped open, and his face almost turned white. I guess it made him think of Isabel and who she was with, not him.

Ted started drinking a lot. He would buy $70 bottles of wine and drink the whole bottle or two by himself at night. I really didn't want to sit around and drink with him. I had better things to do, especially watch the kids. He told me that both his grandfathers were alcoholics, his father was an alcoholic, his brother was an alcoholic, and he was too. I told him he had a choice not to be like them, but he didn't care.

I was embarrassed every recycling day because Ted's wine bottles took up three recycling bins. I used to try to cover them up with the other bins so the neighbors couldn't see them. He was spending a lot of money on wine.

Ted got in a terrible Jet Ski accident one day and came home with his face all bloody and with cuts all over his face. He went straight into the bathroom and wouldn't let me come near him. I was just trying to help. I asked him what happened, and he said he must have hit something that was right below the waterline, and he couldn't see it. We had just had three hurricanes come through, and he could have been telling me the truth. I thought he might have been drugged out, but he went to work the next day, looking like a punching bag. I always loved his motivation, but then again, Isabel was there.

He got in a bad habit of going out on the boat late at night by himself after the rest of us were asleep. I told him it was not a good idea, but he didn't listen to me. He ended up in somebody else's lakefront at about 3:00 a.m. and then woke up. Thank God none of the neighbors saw him. That would have been another tidbit to add to all the gossip.

When I was cleaning his bedroom—I only slept there when he wanted sex, which I didn't enjoy anymore—I found a prescription for Ted written by Isabel. I also found prescriptions written for Ted's mother and brother, all for narcotics. Isabel and Ted were writing the prescriptions so they could use them. That was illegal. I wanted to say something but just kept my mouth shut.

I decided to go to my gynecologist and get myself tested for STDs. I didn't want to catch anything from the slut, Isabel. At times, I felt like I was being paid back for all the poor choices I had made before I married Ted. Now I knew how Landon had felt when I cheated on him. The only difference was that I never stayed with one person very long, and we didn't have kids.

I went to a Catholic priest, who was recommended to me by a friend. He was a mental health counselor. When I told him my story about Isabel and Mark and the drugs, he told me Ted had ruined Mark. I told him that I didn't think that way because my God was a mighty God, and He was stronger than any situation. Mark had a wall of protection around him, and God would never fail. The Catholic counselor just looked at me.

I finally decided I needed to be on an antidepressant. I really didn't want to go on medicine, but I couldn't live the way I was living anymore. I felt stuck. I had four kids to take care of, and it would be difficult to watch them go back and forth to be with him for shared custody. I didn't trust my kids with their own father. I knew God was with me, but I just wanted to try the medical approach also.

One of my friends told me she saw Ted and Isabel at the gym across town. I assumed they started going there so they wouldn't be as obvious. I went there the next day after Ted got off work, and they were both there, working out together. I confronted both of them, and Ted told me to go away because I was ruining his workout. I told them both that what they were doing was wrong, and it was affecting both families in a very negative way. They didn't care who they hurt, not even their own children.

I found out later from one of Isabel's ex-friends that Isabel liked kinky sex. I guess the kinky sex and drugs were what was keeping them together. The same ex-friend also told me that Isabel was suspected of having kinky sex with another one of her ex-friend's husband. It just never ended.

The antidepressant did seem to help me cope better. I still went to the gym a lot and found a good church. I started getting closer and closer to God. Jesus was becoming more and more real to me. He was the only one I could hold on to and trust. I just had to accept the fact that Ted wanted me as his wife and Isabel as his girlfriend.

I was sure Ted was telling his family how horrible I was. Ted would take his nurses over to his mother's for lunch and not include me. It really hurt my feelings. I was the one who suggested she move closer to us in the first place. Anthony, his brother, was still living with his mom and still drinking.

One day, I decided I wasn't going to take the antidepressant anymore. Ted had been giving me an extra $1,000 a month to stay on it. I guess he felt like he had more control of me by giving me extra money and keeping me on a drug.

I went off the medicine cold turkey. You were really supposed to wean yourself off it by tapering off slowly. I just wanted to get it over with, even though I would miss the $1,000 play money. I was sick as a dog for three days straight. The kids were in school most of the day, and

I got my friends to take Abigail for me. I was so nauseated and dizzy that I couldn't get out of bed easily.

I talked to my minister while I was lying in bed. I told him the whole story. He was such a good listener, and he helped me get through the withdrawal stage. I prayed and prayed to God to help me hear what He wanted me to do next.

I got a job at a nursing home at night so I could be home during the day. Melissa was home at night, and she was older now, and I trusted her. She had always been more mature than her age. I got caught up on a lot of my nursing skills because the nursing home was like a mini hospital. We had colostomies, diabetics, feeding tubes, a few cancer patients with morphine pumps, a quadriplegic, breathing treatments, IV therapy, Foley bags, just about everything.

They made me the night supervisor because I was the only RN working there. The rest were LPNs, but they had been there longer than I had, and I asked them questions when I wasn't sure about something. I worked with a really smart black nurse and a Puerto Rican guy. I enjoyed both of them.

I also enjoyed making my own money again. It boosted up my worn-down self-esteem, plus it was a Christian workplace. That made all the difference in the world. We had a police patrol every hour to watch the place for us, so I felt safe. One night, some guy off the streets tried to get in, and we immediately called for help. They were there in a few minutes. That was the kind of policeman I liked.

The Illness

TED CAME HOME FROM THE GYM ONE day, complaining that he couldn't lift as much weight as he usually did. He had been on steroids for quite a while now and was used to lifting heavy weights to keep his muscles big. He said he felt like his arms were getting weaker. Then he said he felt like something was poking him all the time all over his body. He said it felt like someone was jabbing him with pencils. It was all very strange, and I could tell he was getting concerned about it.

He started having difficulty breathing and went to a friend of his who was a pulmonary specialist. He suggested we have our water tested for arsenic. Apparently, arsenic in a water system could cause many health issues, including lung cancer and cardiovascular effects.

Ted and I both got tested to see if we had arsenic in our bodies, and the results accidentally got faxed to his office instead of to our home. Somebody at the office saw the faxed information, and then a rumor got started around town that I was sneaking arsenic into Ted's food, and that was why he was having his symptoms. How low was that? I was furious, and when I heard who was spreading it, I let her know how absurd that was and how I didn't appreciate her gossiping, especially about something that wasn't true.

Ted started losing weight and having difficulty swallowing. He had to use a straw to drink, and his food had to be soft and cut into small pieces. It was very obvious that something was drastically wrong. He started getting to the point where it was difficult for him to use his arms at all. He had two of his nurses, the ones I liked, actually doing the work in his office as he told them what to do. It was scary, and quite frankly, I didn't know if it was legal.

Finally, he realized that he just couldn't handle the workload anymore. He had to quit. Isabel saw his patients. That was the only good thing she did for our family. He put out ads for a partner in his business, knowing he would have to sell out. At first, there were no prospects, so we waited. He would still go into the office and check on the business.

One day, Ted and I got into an argument about Isabel. Since he couldn't use his arms, he pushed me around with his shoulders. Since he was still 200 pounds and I was 108 pounds, he could overpower me. He kept spitting in my face, and after the seventh time, I spit back. I felt really bad doing it, but he wouldn't stop. He kept following me around.

After I spit back, he got very angry with me and pushed me down on the couch with his shoulders and lay down on top of me. I tried to push him off, but he was so heavy that I couldn't get him off. He was like dead weight.

Finally, I gathered my strength and pushed as hard as I could. He stumbled off me and skinned his nose on the wall. Then he sat down on the couch, called his mommy, and told her to come over. I told him not to involve her, and I didn't want her in our house. She had already called me demon possessed and told me never to come over to her house again. I was convinced by now that Ted was bad-mouthing about me to his family and glorifying Isabel. They thought she was wonderful, only they didn't know the whole story about the affair or the drugs.

When I saw his mom and brother, Nita and Anthony, walking in our front door, uninvited by me, I was very annoyed. I knew they were up to no good. Nita came straight up to me and started waving her hands in front of my face like a crazy woman. Then she stuck a camera in my face. I didn't know what she was thinking, but I asked her why she brought the camera.

It was just an automatic response for me to push it out of my face as anyone would have done. When I pushed it out of my face, she lost her balance and fell backwards. I immediately apologized and told her I was sorry she lost her balance, and I would never have had that happen on purpose. We were all stunned.

The next thing that happened also caught me by surprise. Anthony smashed my face with his fist. He was an overweight alcoholic, who was bigger than Ted. I flew across the kitchen, and thankfully, I landed on a box that had blankets in it. I knew that God had that box there for me;

otherwise, I would have hit my head on the floor and had a much worse head injury. Ted had already pushed me onto the cement a week earlier, and my head was bleeding. I had a huge knot on my head, and it was embarrassing when my hairdresser asked me how I got it. I lied about it.

My face was on fire from the pain, and my head was pounding. I almost blacked out from the dizziness. I lay there for a few minutes and heard Nita ask if I was gone yet. Ted just stood there and didn't say a word. They couldn't have cared less about me. I could have been knocked out cold.

I got up and grabbed my car keys and theirs. I threw their keys into the lake just far enough that they would have to wade in the water to get them but close enough that they could see them. Our lake was spring-fed and very clear.

Once I got in my car and looked at my face, I was horrified. I looked like I had been mugged. I started driving down the road and had actually forgotten that there was a police station nearby. I was so traumatized that I really didn't know what to do. I ran into the police station, and they could tell by my face that I had been hit. I told them where I lived, and they followed me back home.

Everyone was still there, and I told the cops I wanted Anthony arrested for hitting me. They asked me if he lived there, and I said, "No, but he was the one who hit me." They said, since he didn't live there, they couldn't arrest him, but they would arrest Ted. I said I didn't want Ted arrested because he was sick. They said they had to arrest someone, and since Ted lived there, he was the one. The whole situation didn't make sense to me. They ended up taking Ted to jail, and I felt terrible about the whole situation. I tried to get some information about what the laws were for domestic violence, but neither the police station nor the courthouse could help me. It was very frustrating. Mark and Adam were not there, but they said they would have beaten the crap out of Anthony if they had been there. All three of them got restraints against me because they said I was such a violent person. Everybody there knew Nita fell and that Anthony beat my face.

I went to a doctor friend of mine to have my face checked out. It was embarrassing sitting in the waiting room and telling my story to the doctor. He said I had three bones broken in my face, and hopefully, they would heal on their own, or I would need to have surgery. I thanked him for seeing me and prayed that my bones would heal. Thank God they did. I still had to walk around town with my face all swollen and bruised but tried not to go out too much. I lied and told people I had run into a pole. They knew I was lying. Several years later I had to have a tooth removed that was cracked because of the impact from Anthony's fist.

Ted was out of jail the next day and moved into a hotel room down the road from our house. The kids and I would visit him. He decided to drop the restraint, realizing how stupid it was. Isabel would go over there every day after work. I got this information from one of the nurses at his office, who had kept me informed all along.

One day, I went to visit him, and he was actually reading a Christian book on his Kindle. I was so surprised and happy about it, especially since he and Isabel had both been reading Buddhist books. I gave him a Christian CD, hoping he would listen to it. There was hope for everybody, and I still prayed for him.

I told Ted that I couldn't live married to him while he was still seeing Isabel. I had asked him several times to get rid of her. I told him to file for divorce because I wasn't going to. He asked me why I wanted a divorce, and I couldn't believe he didn't understand why. I wanted to say, "Because you have been cheating on me for six years and doing drugs with our son.", but I just decided to take the high road and keep my mouth shut. He was a lost soul, and I felt sorry for him.

He moved in with his mom and brother, but that didn't last long because Anthony's lazy, alcoholic lifestyle irritated Ted. His mom lived in a retirement community, and Ted bought his own house there down the road from her.

Ted had told me he was a heroin addict the night before I told him to file for divorce. At first, I didn't believe him and thought he was kidding. Then it all made sense to me that he and Mark were both doing heroin. I hated him for how he had abused his own son. It had filtered down to Adam, who knew that Mark was doing drugs. Now I had a sick husband and two sons with drug problems. I couldn't let them be together, but how could I stop it?

We decided to send Mark to one more rehab. He seemed to be doing better there, so I tried not to worry about him. At least he was away from his father. Melissa had gone to college and dropped out to help take care of Ted in his new house. Ted had spent most of his time with the boys and sports before the drugs took over, so I was glad Melissa got a chance to be with her father. I would rather have had it under different circumstances, of course.

- ❖ I got a lawyer in a town nearby, who was recommended to me, and he got a lawyer from the same town. I kind of resented the fact that Ted's lawyer was a family lawyer and had no children. How could he possibly relate to a family situation in a divorce?
- ❖ Then Ted asked me if I wanted to get a divorce with no lawyers. I thought he was out of his mind. I had stopped trusting and respecting him for a long time. There was no way I wasn't going to have a lawyer. When I said no, he got a second lawyer. I couldn't believe he would do that and why. The second one was really aggressive and didn't consider the children either. I wondered what was wrong with both of them and Ted.
- ❖ We finally realized that Ted had ALS, also called Lou Gehrig's disease. Ted told me it was a disease where your body becomes chemically imbalanced, and half the people have personality changes and impairments with cognitive thinking. Yes, he had said some crazy things to me, but he had been cheating on me way before he had any symptoms of the disease. I started thinking that if it really was a chemically imbalanced disease, with all the drugs he had been doing, he could have thrown his body into that state and actually contributed to getting the disease.
- ❖ Ted's second attorney got him a five-year plan for health insurance and nothing for the children. I couldn't believe Ted would be that selfish, as well as his lawyers. I was fit to be tied. I ended up paying $1,600 a month for our health insurance through my extended health care from my work.
- ❖ When time came for the divorce court proceeding, I had wanted to keep it between Ted and me and not have the kids involved. I asked Melissa to watch Abigail for me and made sure Adam was taken care of. Mark was out of the rehab by now, even though we had wanted him to stay longer.
- ❖ When I arrived at the courthouse and went upstairs to the courtroom, I looked up, and Mark and Melissa were sitting in the waiting room with Ted and his two attorneys. They were

all dressed up like they were going to church. I couldn't believe it. I was in shock, and my heart sank.

❖ Ted had obviously told Mark and Melissa about what time the proceedings were and asked them to be there with him. They had kept it a secret from me that they had planned to be there. It was so typical of Ted to do something like that, and I was ticked off at Mark and Melissa also. They had basically lied to me by not telling me they were going to be there. I hate being lied to. Ted and Mark had been lying to me for way too long.

❖ They both came over to talk with me for a short time, and I told them I had wanted this to be between their father and me only. They didn't say anything, but I could tell they felt torn. They went back to sit with their dad. My heart was broken, and I just really didn't want my life to be so messed up.

Ted and I and the lawyers went into the room before the judge. I was so sad and angry at the same time. I looked across the table at Ted, who used to be so handsome and healthy looking. His long wavy blonde hair was now thinned out and gray. His muscular build was now very thin and pathetic. He just sat there in his wheelchair and said nothing.

I felt sorry for him, mainly because God had given him everything. He had a beautiful family, a beautiful house, and a great career. He threw it all away for one self-centered, lost woman and drugs. Look at him now. The choices we make decide our fate. All he had to do was repent and ask God to forgive him. He was near the end of his journey, and I prayed for his soul.

There is a 10 percent chance of inheriting ALS, but I liked to think of it as a 90 percent chance of not inheriting it. I reminded the boys that the more they did drugs, the more they were chemically altering their body, and that was exactly what their father did.

I told Mark and Melissa that they had basically lied to me about going to the court. They should have told me they were going to be there. I told them I couldn't live with any more lying and that they would both have to find another place to live. It broke my heart, but I couldn't accept the lying.

I talked to my pastor about it, and he said it was not uncommon for the children to side with the weaker parent. I hadn't thought about it that way, but in my mind, Ted had become the weak person when he started doing the drugs. Now he just looked weaker because he was so sick and pathetic looking.

God made me stronger and stronger and is still by my side. I never could have made it through the hell I went through without His help. Jesus was and still is my rock and my refuge.

Mark and Melissa got an apartment together in town. Both of them helped take care of Ted. Ted had narcotics at his house, which were now considered legal for him because he was ill. I really didn't want Mark over there, and he had ADD, so he decided to get a job someplace else.

I decided to put the house up for sale and hired a realtor. The realtor's brother had actually lived in our house before us, and she had sold it to us. I had prayed about selling the house and asked God to please help us find a house we liked just as much as this one. I knew he would find the perfect house for us.

I was out walking our dogs, Lancelot and Guinevere. We called them Lance and Guin. They were golden retrievers. One of our neighbors, who lived down the street on the smaller lake, was also walking his dog. He asked me how things were going with the house. I told him two people had looked at it but no offers. I told him I would probably rent somewhere when we sold it.

He told me he was interested in the house. He had been friends with the man who owned it before we did, who ended up passing away later. He wanted to know if I would be interested in trading houses with him and would like to show it to me.

I said okay, mainly out of curiosity, and I wasn't showing my house very much. I went to look at his house the next day and had never liked the outside. The house was rather plain, and she had potted plants all over the yard. It looked like it needed a lot of work.

When I walked in the front door, however, the view was gorgeous. I liked it even more than the house we were living in. There was a panoramic view of the entire lake, and it was on a hill and closer to the lake. It felt like we were right on top of the lake. The house we were living in had a lot of land between us and the lake.

We went upstairs—our other house was one story—and I fell in love with the house. The bedrooms were twice as big as our other bedrooms, and the view of the lake from the lakeside bedroom picture window was breathtaking. The entire upstairs was perfect for the kids, with a television area also. I didn't like the white carpet, but I could replace that with wood. I would definitely have to do some remodeling, but the view would be worth it.

Zach, our neighbor who wanted to trade houses with us, had money in citrus and could have afforded to pay our asking price for our house. We had put a lot of remodeling into it, and they hadn't in their house. He got his fancy real estate lawyer to come up with a price that he said was just as fair because of the market prices going up and down over the past five years on both of our houses. I wasn't real happy with the deal, but I got enough money to pay off the mortgage and do most of the remodeling I wanted to. It would also be less of a change for the kids to be able to stay in the same neighborhood on the lake.

We packed up, and it took me forever just getting my favorite art pieces down the street. I wanted to personally take care of my stained glass lamps and other items I had gotten from our decorator.

We got ready to bring our two boats and Jet Ski down, and to my surprise, there was no dock. I had been so overwhelmed while looking at the house that I failed to notice that they didn't have a dock. I couldn't believe that they had lived there for twenty years and didn't have a dock. Thankfully, Zach let me keep the boats and jet ski at our previous house till we got our dock built.

It turned out to be a nightmare when I discovered that they had a cheap water system and no water softener. Even the man who sold them the system told me Zach was a penny-pincher. The well water had so much sulfur in it that I had to get a new water system and two new air conditioners. One of the old air conditioners leaked through the ceiling, and I had to get the bathroom dry walled, so I just remodeled the whole bathroom. I remodeled the master bathroom to actually have a bathtub and shower in it rather than a closet.

I paved the driveway and pool area, put in a jacuzzi, and did all new landscaping. We put decorative awnings on the outside windows, put up shutters, and painted inside and outside. I got a picture window in my bedroom and French doors to open up to the pool. I tried not to be bitter toward Zach for taking advantage of my situation. I just thanked God for helping us find a house that we liked so much. I had no bad memories of Ted in this house either, and we had a new start. I felt very blessed to be living in my "glass house", that my dad had told me I needed to live in.

The men who worked on the house were something else. One of them, who did most of the re flooring, had two of his sons helping him. He had been a youth minister when he was younger and was always flirting with me and quoting scriptures at the same time. Thank God he wasn't my type. After he finished the work at the house, he sent me the filthiest text message I have ever received, telling me how he would be the best man I had ever been with and using other vulgar words. I texted him back and asked him if he had forgotten who God was or if was he on drugs. He tried to apologize, but it was too late.

I stupidly went out with the guy who built our dock, only because he was a friend of a friend of mine. We had nothing in common, and I was bored the whole time. We had a fire pit built, and when this guy asked me out, I just said no. The worst one was the energy-control guy. He did my solar power system and picture window. He asked me to show him my boobs. That was the last straw. I didn't want any more men working on my house.

I called my decorator I hired at our other house, and she finished the rest of the work. Her rate was expensive, but she did a great job. I loved my house and felt very blessed to be there.

Now it was just Adam, Abigail, and me living in our new house. I still had to take Abigail to school in the morning after I got off work. One morning, I was so sleepy that I ran into a pole in the middle of a fork in the road. I had fallen asleep for a brief moment and immediately woke up when I hit the pole. Strangely, one of my old boyfriends from high school just happened to be driving by when the accident happened. He came over and recognized me and offered to help. He called the police, and he was a nice one. He told me to go home and get some sleep and didn't give me a ticket. It was also good to see Luke, my old boyfriend.

I had to get babysitters to watch the kids for me when I worked because I didn't want them alone at night. Melissa had always been home to watch them. One night, they called me in, and I couldn't find a babysitter, so I asked Melissa if she could come over for the night. She already had plans, so I reluctantly asked Mark. I told him to please be responsible and mature while watching them. He agreed.

When I got home the next morning, the first thing I saw were some beer cans lying in the yard. Then I came inside, and there were bags of beer cans in the trash and a bong and some ashes all over the kitchen.

There was obviously a party at the house while I was working. There was vomit on the back porch rug, and it looked like brown rice. Adam had brown rice for dinner that night. He was passed out in his bed upstairs, and so was Mark. I was ticked.

I woke Mark up and started yelling at him. He said that he had fallen asleep early and didn't even know Adam had anybody over. I knew he was lying, but there was nothing I could do about it. Adam was still hung over, and it was a waste of my time to even attempt to scold him. That was the night that I put in my notice at work. Someone had also stolen my favorite expensive diamond cross out of my bathroom drawer. I was so disappointed and unhappy about it.

I started working at Holy Shepherd, the private school that Abigail still attended. I had to quit my night job. I worked there part-time days and loved it. The kids were so fun, and no one was really that sick. It was a lot better than working with sick and dying adults.

Abigail was growing up to be a beautiful young lady and was popular with her friends. She had pool parties and sleepovers, and we went tubing on the lake. We used the boat more because the jet ski only carried three people. She was still playing soccer and seemed well-adjusted. Ted had spent the least amount of time with her since she was the youngest. Melissa would come over and take her to see her dad.

Isabel was still working at the office and got sued. She stupidly was treating a guy she met at the gym. She put him on a medicine that was contraindicated for another health issue that he had. Thank God Ted's malpractice insurance paid for it. I thought, *What a stupid thing to do.*

I knew that Ted's illness had affected all the children in a very negative way. Adam was still struggling to finish high school. It made me so sad to see such a good mind go to waste, but I knew he was grieving. Melissa got tired of living with Mark and asked me if she could come back home. I said yes, and I really was happy to have her back. Then, of course, Mark wanted to come home also. I said yes, and I knew I would have more stress with him home, but I still loved my children no matter what. I knew that they were very distraught about their dad and were confused about what to do when he was trying to get them to favor him.

I would e-mail Ted and tell him that he and Isabel were both committing adultery and that it was even worse having the kids know about it. He asked me three times why we got the divorce. I felt like he was just stupid, or the disease had really affected his mind. He wouldn't let me see him, even though I went over there several times. I think he actually felt guilty as he should have, but I also think that he was still vain enough that he didn't want me to see how much he was physically deteriorating. Adam said he didn't want to go over there anymore because it made him too sad. He started to cry, and my heart was broken.

We finally got a doctor who was interested in working at the office with the option to buy. His name was Dr. Melvin Toste. His wife's name was Greeda. They both lived up to their names. He was kind of a pansy, and she was very greedy and money hungry. At first, I liked them; but when they heard about Ted and Isabel from the town gossipers, they both told me they didn't want to get "involved." It really kind of hurt my feelings because I never said anything to them about the affair. They could have just kept their mouths shut.

The "affair" must have made an impression on Greeda because she took over the office and even kept her kids there after school. Either she didn't trust Melvin or Isabel or she didn't trust both. She chased most of the staff away. They didn't want to work with her because she was so bossy. Isabel and one other nurse stayed.

The one nurse who stayed there was a friend of Isabel's. Her name was Dana. She told me later that Melvin had complained to her that Greeda wouldn't give him blow jobs. It sounded like Dana stuck around for a reason.

Dr. Toste hired another nurse practitioner and bought five other practices. Greeda opened a massage parlor with cosmetic procedures available through another nurse practitioner. They sold the building and bought another bigger one down the street. The doctor who had owned that building had been arrested for selling narcotics to undercover agents. Melvin and Greeda just couldn't make enough money to keep themselves happy.

Ted continued to live in the same house near his mom and brother. Melissa and Mark helped take care of him when the paid caretakers needed relief. One of the caretakers was a guy, Drake. He had a huge crush on Melissa, but she had no interest in him. He became friends with Mark and me, though. He told me that his father was a drug dealer and used to take him in the car with him while he was dealing. Drake said he didn't want to be anything like his dad and had chosen not to do drugs because of his father. If only my boys had thought like that.

One day, Mark called the family together, and we all sat down in the family room. He told us that Ted had passed away, and all the kids started crying. All I could think about was how sad that he had died without his family there, and it was of his own choosing. I was sure he thought about all he had done and had some remorse. Drake told me later that Ted didn't even want Isabel there at the end, and for some reason, that made me feel better. Maybe he didn't want to see her face as a reminder of the bad choices he had made. I prayed for his soul.

Life after Ted

THE FUNERAL WAS A NIGHTMARE. IT WAS at the Catholic church where Ted went with his mother once she moved into town. It was also where I had talked to the priest who said Ted had ruined Mark. It wasn't one of my favorite places in town.

As I mentioned before, I was sure Ted had been bad-mouthing about me to his mom, brother, and sister. They tried to keep me from going to the funeral, but there was no way I wasn't going to be there for my children, especially Abigail and Adam. They were thirteen years old and sixteen years old. I wasn't the bad guy, but I guess they had to blame everything on somebody, and that was me.

I went anyway. I talked to the priest and told him the whole story. I told him I was coming, and I knew they wouldn't make a scene in front of the people at church. The kids went separately, and I came later. When I got to the church, I sat in the second row behind my kids. It was made very clear that the front row seats were not for me. I sat with four of my closest friends, who were there to give me emotional support. They already knew how badly Ted's family had treated me.

I was so sad for my children. All I wanted to do was hold Abigail in my arms and hold Adam's hand and tell them how much I loved them and that everything was going to be okay. I knew everyone there knew about Isabel, except maybe his patients. I really couldn't have cared less. My friends knew that I wasn't in the wrong. They told me Isabel was sitting in the back of the church.

Ted had been cremated, and they made Adam hold the ashes. I thought that was very cruel. Melissa was twenty-one years old, and Mark was twenty-three. I felt like Mark should have been the one to hold them. Adam was crying the whole time. It made me cry. It was a very cold funeral, and none of his friends got up to talk. Two of his caretakers were basically the only speakers, and I felt like it was just a very sad and unorganized last-minute ceremony. I prayed that his soul would be in heaven. His mom told me later that he had a glow around him right before he died. I was thinking that he finally asked Jesus into his heart, just like the thief on the cross next to Jesus when he was crucified. I would like to see him there and our whole family reunited with Jesus. It is never too late.

After the funeral, I had a chance to talk to some of the people whom I liked there. Our pastor came, who knew Ted before he started going to the Catholic church with his mom. It was good to see some of Ted's old staff there. They had sympathetic looks on their faces. I was glad when it was over.

He died on Valentine's Day. Now every Valentine's Day is ruined for all of us. I used to decorate the house on Valentine's Day but thought it might upset the children and make them think of their dad more. I was going to decorate it this year, though. It is past time to move forward. I just try to keep the good memories.

It tore up the kids, each in a different way. Mark finished junior college and decided to work at a job laying decorative concrete floors and working at a health food store. He even got a job in another city in a store that sold razors for facial shaving. None of them lasted long. He had another motorcycle and drove it like a maniac.

Adam went crazy with drugs and couldn't finish high school. He started taking online classes to try to finish his diploma qualifications so he could play football up East. He had gotten a partial scholarship there if his grades were good enough. I took him to a doctor, who prescribed a medicine for him that was supposed to block the "high" feeling from the drugs that he was taking. It seemed to be helping him.

Mark started dating a Mexican girl, Queenie; we called her that because she acted like a prima donna. They fought all the time, and no one in our family liked her. Her own sister had told Mark that she was supposed to be on medication because she was bipolar. She also told him that Queenie was supposed to be going to anger management classes but didn't go. I tried to be nice to her at first because she was an ICU nurse and thought she had to have something good about her.

Mark and she had a huge fight one night. Mark put a gun in his mouth, and she called the cops. He ended up in the lockdown unit in the hospital. When I went to pick him up the next day, the nurse told me that he was the third boyfriend that week who had been called in by their girlfriends. She said she thought maybe this was a new trend. I was upset by the whole situation. It was like they both had fatal attractions to each other.

I didn't know what to think. If I had been Queenie, I might have done the same thing. Nurses tend to think alike in cases like that. Then I started thinking that Mark had been dove hunting when he was younger, and he knew guns really well. I asked him if he had the safety on, and he said yes. They were both being overly dramatic.

When he got out, they were still seeing each other. It got to be such a bad situation that I really didn't want them in the house anymore. I told Mark the family didn't want her in our house. One of my friends, who was married to a cardiologist, told me Queenie was talking about me to her husband at the hospital, and he told her he didn't want to hear it. What a poor soul. I prayed for her.

Mark and Adam were both crazy on drugs. I just didn't know what drugs they were on. I would find cotton swabs, needles, syringes, and spoons with white or blue residue on them hidden in drawers or under the bed. I felt like I was in a junkie's house, which I basically was. I felt trapped in my own house, living in a foreign world, having to learn a foreign language. My journey was taking me down a pathway that I didn't understand and hated. The boys would fall asleep in front of the television for hours. I prayed to God to help me know what to do next, falling on my knees in desperation.

The final straw was when they started stealing money from my wallet. They actually went to my computer and got into my bank account. Adam pawned my father's rifle that he had given him, and it had sentimental value to me. I was so angry at him for doing that. He also pawned a very expensive gold chain that he had bought. I found the gold chain, but I never found the rifle. I wanted out. I couldn't handle my life anymore.

They were costing me a fortune on food because they both were big and ate a lot. They also lied to me over and over again about needing money to get a pill that kept them off the harder drugs. I stupidly believed them. I was desperate and started getting depressed again. Jesus was the only one who kept me afloat.

Mark and Adam got in a huge fight in our backyard. Adam had been drinking, and he was a horrible drinker. It made him go crazy. He got a hammer and tried to hit Mark with it several times. He was so wasted. Even though he was bigger than Mark, Mark hit him in the face, and Adam fell to the ground. He was so angry, and after he got up, he started running after Mark. Mark had called Queenie to pick him up earlier, and the minute she got here, I told her and Mark to leave. I tried to get Adam to calm down. I knew he was angry about his father's death and angry at Mark. My heart was so sad for them.

Adam drove over to Queenie's house, hammered her truck several times, left big dents in her truck, and then drove off. I was concerned that he would get in a wreck just driving his truck. His angels were driving for him and protecting him from getting pulled over by the cops. I told Queenie I would pay to have her truck fixed and to please not call the cops. She agreed, and after getting two different estimates for having the truck repaired, I had her truck looking good again.

I had been supporting all four kids for three years now. I was spending $2,000 a month on food alone. The boys ate so much, and I fixed a big dinner every night. I was also paying for health insurance, clothing, car insurance, and all the bills. It was stressful, but at least I had enough money to keep us going for a while. God always provided for us.

It was difficult for me to understand why Ted had made his sister trustee for the kids' funds. She hardly knew them, and even Ted had told me she was a miser. She had told me that Ted was selfish. I guess they knew each other pretty well. The will specified that the kids were to get the first third of their inheritance at twenty-five years old, then thirty years old for the second third, and finally thirty-five years old for the last third. How was I supposed to support all of them for that long? Abigail was thirteen years old, Adam was sixteen years old, Melissa was twenty-one years old, and Mark was almost twenty-three years old when Ted died. Legally, if Susan, his sister, didn't give Abigail any money till she was twenty-five years old, we would have to wait for twelve years. It was so unfair and mean for him to do that.

I kept praying that Susan and Nita, my mother-in-law, would get closer and closer to God. Then they would love themselves better and in return love others better, including me. I wrote them both a letter and asked them to please forgive me for whatever I did to make them hate me so. Nita was very sweet about it. She said she forgave me but didn't know what for. She was getting older, now ninety-three years old and in remission from cancer. Susan said she didn't want to have anything to do with me and to never communicate with her again unless absolutely necessary. I thought, *Well, at least I tried and continued to pray that they both get closer to God.*

Mark turned twenty-five years old, and Susan gave him his first third of his inheritance. It was more than $100,000. Mark was still doing drugs and never should have gotten that money. The will also specified that if any of the kids were on drugs, the trustee had the right to withhold the funds. I had already told Susan that Mark, Isabel, and Ted were doing drugs together. She said I was lying. Anyway, Mark spent all his inheritance on drugs and stuff in nine months. I was furious that she even gave it to him. If I had been the trustee, I would not have done it that way.

Then a miracle happened. Susan e-mailed me and told me she got a "feeling" that she should make me the trustee for the kids. She said the "feeling" came around Christmas. I knew it was God speaking to her so loudly that she finally heard Him. She had tried to get the second person on the list to be trustee, but he didn't want to do it. I had to call his eighty-year-old mother to get him to write a formal letter stating his decision not to be trustee. I couldn't believe he wouldn't answer my phone calls about it. Finally, he sent the paperwork in so we could proceed with the transfer of trusteeship to me.

I finally got to be trustee for my kids. Better late than never. It was the only right thing to do. Susan didn't even give Melissa enough money to buy a car, so I paid for it. Susan knew Melissa was living with me, so she took advantage of that fact. It took several months for the transfer to transpire, but I finally got everything transferred to my accountant, who was also affiliated with financial planning. I trusted him and his secretary, and they were both Christians with kids of their own.

Melissa decided she wanted to go to Chicago with her best friend from private school. She wanted to take a year long culinary school course at a very reputable school. She loved to cook and bake, so I said yes. She was having a blast until her best friend, Crystal, got into a relationship with another girl. It wasn't just a friendship; it was a lover relationship. It blew Melissa's mind that her best friend since the third grade was gay. Crystal was never home and was always at her new girlfriend's place. Thankfully, God had put two really nice girls in Melissa's pathway. At the last minute of moving up to Chicago, Crystal and Melissa got two roommates from California, who had gone to a Christian college. They basically saved Melissa from having to live in her apartment by herself. They all got along well and became good friends. The father of one of the girls was very wealthy, and he helped them get a much nicer place than they would have had without him.

Melissa moved back home after the culinary course, which she loved, but didn't want to stay in Chicago. She said it had been a lot of fun, and she learned how to cook so many different gourmet dishes from well-known chefs. She just didn't expect her stay to end with her best friend leaving her. Crystal stayed with her new girlfriend. Melissa really didn't want to have anything to do with Crystal after that for quite a while. Thankfully, Melissa decided to forgive Crystal for abandoning her, and they are friends now. She even went up to Chicago to stay with Crystal to celebrate her birthday.

Crystal's mom didn't want to talk about it at first. I talked to her about it and reminded her that several of our mutual friends had gay kids. I freaked out at first over a situation at Holy Shepherd, where Abigail attended. One of the mothers called me up and said that her daughter was approached by a gay girl, Patti, at a slumber party hosted by another mom who also had a gay son. Her daughter was a friend of Abigail's at Holy Shepherd. The mom who called me also called the administration at Holy Shepherd and demanded that Patti be expelled from the school. One thing led to another, and eventually, they both left. It was a huge mess.

I didn't understand the gay world, but I also didn't understand alcoholics or drug abusers. All I know is Jesus came for sinners, not perfect people, and I am certainly not perfect. The world is changing, and God still tells us to love one another. We don't have to agree with their lifestyle, but we are supposed to love others as we love ourselves. Church is really like a hospital, with wounded and hurt people. Whether you admit it or not, we all need healing, each in our own way. Humans are not flawless. Thank God for the great physician, Jesus.

Melissa decided to take some courses at the local junior college and major in nutrition, knowing she would be transferring to a bigger school later. She continued to live with me, and I was happy to have her with us.

Adam was acting crazy again. He totaled his new truck when he was coming around a curve on his way home at five thirty in the morning. He hit a semi, which was pulling out of a residential section near our home. Our neighbor said he actually heard the crash. I didn't hear anything. I got a call from a cop, saying that Adam had been in an accident and that he was in the ER at the local hospital where I had first worked. By the time I got there, they were almost ready to discharge him. His face looked horrible. He had abrasions all over his face, and I hardly recognized him. Thank God he had no internal injuries that they were aware of and no neck or back injuries.

His truck was ruined, and the tow guy said Adam should have been dead from what the truck looked like. His face totally healed with no scarring. He said he didn't see the semi pulling out till he rounded the corner. I thanked God again for saving Adam. His guardian angels covered him during that accident.

As if that wasn't enough drama in our lives, Adam got involved with another girl, Hellen. She met him through an app on the phone, and they got together one night. She was spending the night with a friend, and they both sneaked out of her house. I was at the grocery store when Hellen and her friend came over, and Adam had a guy friend over also. They went for a boat ride on our boat.

Apparently, she got drunk and accused Adam of raping her. There were two other people on the boat with them, so it really didn't make sense. The rape kit ended up negative, so Hellen was obviously lying. When the mother couldn't find the girls, she called the cops, and that was how Adam got in trouble. Hellen and her mother blamed everything on Adam, even though Hellen had contacted Adam first. Adam had just turned eighteen years old, and the girl lied about her age and said she was also eighteen. She was really sixteen years old but had big boobs and looked a lot older, just like how my mother and Mark had looked older than their ages.

I felt it was very unfair that Adam got all the blame. Hellen's mother should have said something about her daughter instigating the meeting in the first place and sneaking out. I truly believed that Hellen would get herself into more trouble with someone else.

Adam got charged with contributing to the delinquency of a minor, even though she lied about her age, and he was barely eighteen years old. I was furious about the whole situation. I called our attorney, and he said he would get Adam out the next morning.

As I have mentioned before, the sheriff and his cops are slime balls. There were a few nice ones. They left Adam in his underwear all night and didn't feed him a thing. This was a 6'4" and a 220-pound kid. I wanted to picket the jail after that and call our local paper about how abusive they were at the jail but decided not to get any more involved. God always made things right, and I believed that what went around came around. Later, in the local newspaper, there were several articles about the sheriff getting sued because of the inferior treatment of inmates. The truth finally came out.

Adam's judge was a little man, Judge Lytledick. I was sure he looked at Adam—who was tall, blonde, and handsome—and took pleasure in putting him on two to three times a week of random drug testing and random alcohol testing with one hundred community hours. Even Adam's probation officer said that was the strictest testing he had ever seen. Judge Lytledick was obviously a jealous, nerdy weasel with authority and the "little man's complex."

I talked to my attorney and told him that I wanted to put Adam in a drug rehab. We had to go through a different judge to get this accomplished. I knew this judge because I had met him at a church where his son was the minister. He had actually sat on our dock at the house while we had a glass of wine. He was a good man, but because I knew him, my attorney told me to wait outside the courtroom while Adam and he went inside with the judge. Otherwise, he might have to disqualify himself since he knew me personally.

I waited outside the door of the courtroom in the waiting room with the rest of the people who were waiting for their turn to go in. I got down on my knees, folded my hands, and prayed to God for the Holy Spirit to take over the courtroom and for Judge Tye, my friend, to hear God's voice and let Adam go to the rehab where he could get some help.

Calvin, our attorney, came out the door with his thumbs up. Yes, Adam could go to the rehab. I was so excited that I got up off my knees and said to everyone there in the waiting room, "If you don't believe in Jesus, you need to because He answers prayers." People started clapping and saying amen. It was awesome. I even had a woman come up to me and ask me to pray with her about her husband. He was on probation, lost his job, and couldn't pay his probation costs. We held hands and asked for God's favor. I really wanted to give her some money, but it would have been rather awkward there.

Later, I had a chance to thank Judge Tye for letting Adam go to the rehab. I went to his son's church again and told him that Adam was my son because he didn't know. I told him that I had prayed that the Holy Spirit would be in the courtroom, and he said he definitely got a feeling that he should let Adam go. I also told him that just putting a kid in jail doesn't help him, but at least giving them a chance for rehab could change their lives. He thanked me for telling him and said he would think about it more with his next cases. It is so nice to know that there are still some fair and honest men in the judicial system.

We took Adam to the rehab. Mark went with me. Mark had been there before and said he should have stayed there longer, and he probably would have benefited more. We drove up to the drop-off in front of the rehab hospital, and some of the techs recognized Mark and started talking to him. Adam got his suitcase out of my car and started looking through Mark's. Mark and I had planned on staying at the beach that night.

Before we knew it, Adam had grabbed Mark's prescription bottle of sleeping pills. Mark had difficulty sleeping and had brought the bottle with him for the night. Mark tried to get them away from him, and the two of them started fighting right there in front of everybody. The techs were just as surprised as I was. Adam swallowed the whole bottle of medicine, and the techs had to break up the fight. Both of them had bloody faces. I was a nervous wreck and just wanted to get out of there. I checked Adam in while they took him into the hospital for detoxification. I felt good about the fact that there were doctors and nurses there to monitor him. They told me later that he slept the whole day and night. Thank God he was okay. The techs who knew Mark said they would take special care of Adam for us.

I was sad when we were leaving because I would miss Adam's good side. Drugs change a person and make them not themselves. Satan and his demons try to destroy people with drugs, but God is stronger, and when we cling to Him, He protects us against temptations. I always tell my kids to choose their friends wisely. I tell them that good people can still make poor choices. We have to be strong and make good choices, even if we have to stop hanging around people we know are not good influences on us.

Mark went up to Canada to a rehab, and they gave him a shot that was supposed to help his cravings for drugs. It was a very nonconventional rehab. He stayed up there for about a month. It was really nice just having the girls at home without the stress of the boys and their drug drama.

It was also nice not to have to worry about them stealing money from me or stealing my jewelry. To this day, I miss my favorite diamond cross. I gave one to my mother-in-law when she started being nice to me. I told her to please will it to one of my girls, and she agreed. I got a locksmith to put a combination lock on my bedroom closet door. I keep my purse and jewelry in there and anything else of value that could be easily stolen. I felt like a burden had been lifted off my shoulders, and I prayed to God that the boys would stay straight.

Mark came home from Canada, but I didn't think it really helped him. He also didn't want to help himself enough. Dana, one of Ted's nurses whom I liked, started coming over to the house with Mark. She told me she was trying to get him to date one of her daughters. She was always giving Ted Christian books and cards and was very pretty for her age. She was probably in her late forties, with pretty skin and long wavy honey-colored hair. I wondered why Ted wasn't more attracted to Dana instead of Isabel.

Well, it turned out that Dana was a drug abuser and had been for years, according to her sister. She was a functional abuser, like Ted and Isabel had been. She was actually doing drugs with Mark and Isabel. She was coming over to my house and dating Mark and lied to me about trying to set him up with her daughter. When I found out the truth about what was going on, I couldn't believe I had been so trusting again. All those years she had worked for Ted, I thought she was the sweetest Christian lady, and what a disappointment to find out that it was all a lie. Dana was old enough to be Mark's mother.

Dana started living with Isabel when she didn't want to live with her boyfriend anymore. I thought, *What a horrible example of a mother she was.* The next thing that happened was Isabel got arrested for possession of five different narcotics in her car and blamed it on Dana. Isabel got put in jail, with a great mug shot on the computer, and lost her nurse practitioner's license. She also was put on five years' probation and one hundred hours of community work.

Dana became an informant for less sentence time, and Mark said she is a dead woman if she gets anywhere near our town. She has a price on her head if any of the people she dealt with see her.

Both Isabel and Dana worked for Dr. Melvin Toste, and he made sure he fired them quickly. He told me, when he bought Ted's building, that he didn't want to get involved; but what he didn't realize was that, by keeping Isabel there, he became involved. The cops had to do an investigation of the office staff. What went around came around.

Mark decided he needed to get out of our redneck little town and get away from all the bad influences he had made contacts with. He made the decision to go out West and somehow got accepted to the university out west where I had gone. I loved it there and told him he could go as long as his grades were good.

Now that I had control of the trust for the kids, I decided I would set up an account where I could send Mark small amounts of cash for his bills, and I paid his apartment rent with his trust checks. We had gone out earlier to look for an apartment and found a nice one away from the younger kids. It was a better environment for an older student. Mark was almost twenty-seven years old when he went out there. He would have transferred as a junior, but some of his classes from the junior college didn't transfer. He had a beautiful view of the mountains, and they had an indoor pool and a small gym room. I met the manager of the apartments, Gwen. She was about my age and very nice.

Mark asked two of his friends to help him move with a big moving truck. It was utter chaos as usual. Mark had gotten his dates wrong for the first day of school and had to hustle at the last minute to find a truck and get everything packed. He wanted me to go with him and drive the truck, but that was the last thing I wanted to do. I didn't want to drive all the way to Colorado and leave the girls alone, especially Abigail.

Thankfully, one of the guys helping Mark volunteered to drive the moving van for me. He was already experienced in driving trucks at night for his job and had just been laid off. That was perfect timing. God saved me again.

I paid him to drive for me and also paid for his flight back. He said they stopped him and made him wait while they inspected his clothing and backpack. He was a cute muscular black kid, with crazy-looking hair. His name was Augie. I told him how much I appreciated him doing this for us.

He turned out to be a really nice guy and later a friend to me. He told me that Mark and the other friend who helped Mark move were both on meth while they were packing everything into the moving van. Augie said he wasn't about to do that "kind of shit." I liked him even more after that. He got drunk one night, though, and asked me if I would be interested in a younger boyfriend. He called me a MILF. I was a little embarrassed but told him not really. I knew he was drunk and he called me up later and apologized.

I was glad Augie told me about the meth because I wondered why Mark was acting so crazy while they were packing. I thought he was just anxious about moving to Colorado. At the same time, though, I was really ticked off that they did that. I didn't want the other kid at our house after Mark left. He had offered to help me around the house if I needed help. I didn't say anything to Mark about the meth because I didn't want him to know that Augie had told me about it.

Mark called me later and said he was settled in his new apartment and made it to his first day of classes. I reminded him that it was very expensive to pay out of state tuition, and he needed to make good grades. He said he would. He was intelligent and just needed to straighten up and study hard.

Life with Just the Girls at Home

ADAM, IN THE MEANTIME, WAS STILL IN the same rehab. Thank God we had the trust money to pay for all this. Adam got a portion of the money from selling Ted's house and handicapped van. A Christian guy friend of mine had sold Ted's house for me and got a good price for it when there were other houses on the same street that hadn't been sold. I felt like God helped us with the sale. The realtor kind of had a crush on me, but he wasn't my type. I wished I could make myself want to be with him, but I just had to have some attraction there. I actually prayed that God would help me be more attracted to him because he was such a nice guy. We still occasionally texted each other.

It was totally not fair that it cost so much to put your kid in rehab. It would be so awesome if all the states would fund rehabs, and then the abusers could have a better chance of becoming who God wants them to be.

I prayed so hard for Adam to straighten up. I put the full armor of God and the blood of Jesus on him every day. Adam had been such a sweet little boy, and it made me so sad to see what Satan had tried to do to him. When he told me that Mark had given him his first narcotic when he was twelve years old, I was livid. Then I started thinking that Mark had learned this behavior from his father. Ted had done drugs with Mark, so his bad example passed down to Adam. I didn't believe that drug abuse was a disease. Diabetes was a disease. You could have it when you were a kid, or you could eat yourself into diabetes when you were older. You could actually heal yourself from diabetes by eating correctly, losing weight, and exercising. I claimed the generational blessing for my family. With God, all things are possible, and my family will all be Christ followers in the name of Jesus.

Our family had been so happy, and Ted had been a good example of what a father should be before he let the drugs rule his life. I tried to think of the good times we had before the drugs became an issue, but it didn't come easily. I could forgive Ted for cheating on me much easier than for doing the drugs, especially with Mark. I prayed for God to help me be a more forgiving person.

Adam relapsed four times while at the rehab. Each time they called me, my heart sank in despair. I cried and cried, but God always heard me. He was my rock. He kept making me stronger and stronger. I kept praying and never gave up. At least Adam was still alive. I kept telling the boys that God had kept them alive for a reason so they could help others.

While Adam was in the hospital after the fourth relapse, one of his friends, Nick, decided he was going to leave the hospital AMA (against medical advice). He wanted to celebrate his birthday. I had met Nick when I visited Adam and took them both out to lunch. They were living at a halfway house then before the last relapse. Nick was such a sweet kid, and he thanked me over and over again for taking him out to lunch.

Adam told me Nick's mother left his dad for some rich guy, and Nick had found his big brother dead from a drug overdose. My heart just went out to him and his dad. He had been through so much at such a young age.

Adam told me that Nick had asked him to go with him to celebrate his birthday. Thank God Adam said no. I had no doubt that the Holy Spirit kept him in the hospital, where he would be safe. They found Nick dead the next day in his hotel room from a drug overdose. He didn't overdose on purpose. As I mentioned before, the rehabilitated body can't handle the previously used amount of drug of choice. Now Nick's parents had two dead sons from drugs. I felt so sorry for both of them. If Adam had chosen to go with Nick, he might not be alive now. God definitely saved him again.

Adam finally got to the point where he could live in the three-quarter house, then the halfway house, and finally the sober living apartments. While he was there, he met a pretty black girl named Natalie. I was not happy about him dating her at first. She was at the rehab for a DUI instead of drugs, and she was eight years older than Adam.

After a while, I started liking her. She was a Christian, worked out at the gym, was pretty and fit, and had a good job and two years of college. She seemed to really care about Adam, and since she was older, she was a better influence on him than the younger girls had been.

Adam has been going to meetings that teach the twelve-step program and were God centered. I also sent him a Bible that paralleled the twelve steps. He had a regular sponsor, and he was also a sponsor. They all helped each other stay sober, and he said they were a good influence on him. Later, he became a speaker for the new kids entering the rehab.

I look back now at how disappointed I was when Adam ended up in a rehab instead of playing football with his football scholarship. Now I know that God had a much better plan because He knows the big picture of our lives. If Adam had gone to play football without getting help with his drug abuse problem, he would have never made it as a football player and student.

Adam was now attending a well-known college down south in a nice apartment, which overlooked a lake, with the big city in the background. He liked it there because there was more to do for young people than in our small little town. It was too busy for me, but I liked it when I was younger. I kept praying for him every day all day to make good decisions and to choose his friends wisely. I also prayed that God would put people in my kids' lives who would help lead them closer to Christ.

Melissa started school at the local junior college. She also started working at the gym that we had been members at for seventeen years, since we moved from Houston. The original location was across town, and that was where I decided to get my first boob job. I had gel falsies in my bra. After breast-feeding four babies, I had practically no boobs left. I was doing an arm machine where I pushed my arms forward, and one of my falsies fell out. I was so embarrassed and hoped that a huge hunky guy wasn't next to me. Thankfully, it was an old lady, and when she saw it lying on the floor between us, she screamed. I quickly picked it up and hid it under my shirt, praying that nobody else saw it. It was definitely time for a boob job. So I got my first one and was glad I did.

I love the gym to this day. The owners were some of our first friends when we moved from Houston. It is such a great way to de stress and look and feel better at the same time. I always loved seeing Melissa's smiling face behind the front desk to greet everyone as they came in. All my friends kept telling me how pretty she was. She also made some good friends there.

Unfortunately, she started dating a guy who also worked there, Aaron. Melissa always had guy friends but not really a boyfriend. At first, I liked him, but all her friends kept telling me what a jerk he was. Melissa and he ended up breaking up, and it really upset her. She cried for three weeks straight and then finally realized that he wasn't worth it.

Working at the gym was good for her. It helped bring out her people skills and got her more interested in working out. Ted, the boys, and I had always worked out; but Melissa was still interested in dance lessons.

The people who worked out at the gym were a varied group. The older ones usually worked out when I did, and I liked it that way. Lunchtime was the best because all the grunts didn't come in till later. Someone told me that 30 percent of the guys were on steroids. I didn't know how he would know, but there was a rumor that he was selling them to people at the gym. Those kinds of guys really turned me off because of all I went through with Ted and Mark. They were the guys always looking at themselves in the mirror and walking around looking like blown-up muscle man figurines.

There was also a black trainer there. I called him Dog. For some reason, all the wealthy people in town liked to use him as their trainer. Mark and Adam said he was the worst trainer there. He gave me the creeps. He was tall with big shoulders and skinny legs. He had gold teeth, but he told me later that his wife wanted him to get rid of them. I told him he looked much better without them. He was a slime ball. He asked me if I would be interested in doing a ménage à trois with him and his friend who just got a divorce. His wife had been a stripper and ran off with the divorce attorney. It totally grossed me out, and I told him so and asked what his wife would think about that. He said he wasn't married and then made a point later to tell me that he was married. He wouldn't give up, though. He asked me again if I would let him train me for free. I told him, "Thank you, but I like my own workouts."

Melissa remained friends with one of Mark's old girlfriends, Jen. I had let her live with us for a while in our other house when Mark was doing heroin. I knew it wasn't right, but since she didn't have a place to live and didn't do drugs, I thought she would be a good influence on him, and maybe he would quit doing the drugs.

That relationship didn't last long. She ended up having to see a therapist because he drove her so crazy. She got to the point where she would run if he was near her. I totally understood how she felt because I had felt the same way about Ted. I felt guilty bringing Jen into our family drama, but I guess I was desperate at that time. I really thought she could help him, but he didn't want to help himself enough yet.

Jen became a bartender and taught Melissa all the tricks and trades of being a top-notch bartender. Melissa quit working at the gym and started working at a newly opened bar in town. Jen knew the owners, and when Melissa interviewed for the job, they liked her immediately. She worked there on the weekends while she was in school at the junior college. She really liked it and still does and made more money on tips than I ever did as a nurse.

Melissa met a really nice guy, Trey, who was a friend of one of the regulars at the bar where she worked. He was nice-looking, friendly, athletic, and hardworking with a college degree. Motivation and education have always been important to me, I guess because of my dad being that way. He and Melissa seemed to really get along well. They lasted for quite a while and then he got weird like so many guys do, and lost the best girl he would ever get!

Abigail had always been an easy child. She went everywhere with me since she was the baby of three other siblings. I prayed that she would learn some lessons from her older brothers about what not to do and make good choices about who her friends were. She has always been pretty and athletic. She wanted to stay at the private school all the way through since the first grade. She made a lot of friends there. Many moved on to other schools, but her closest friends stayed. I was glad she wanted to stay there because I felt like it was a more controlled environment than public school.

Once Abigail and her friends all turned sixteen years old and could drive, life started changing again. Abigail liked to have her friends over, and I really liked them being over. They would use our boat and swim in the pool or use the fire pit when it was cold enough. I wasn't as concerned about Abigail getting in trouble as I was with Mark and Adam. Melissa had been no problem.

One night, Abigail called me around midnight and told me I needed to meet her at the drugstore down the street. I got there, and her car was parked in the parking lot of the store. A police car was there, and Abigail and one of her girlfriends were in the back of the car. I was totally freaked out.

There were two cops there. One was a jerk, and the other one was really nice. The nice one told me that the store had been broken into several times and that one of the local vendors had called them to let them know there was a single car in the parking lot after the store was closed. The girls were crying. They were only sixteen years old. The trunk of Abigail's car was open, and there was a bottle of liquor and a small amount of pot in a baggie in plain sight. I was so upset and asked her how she got both of them and from who. Of course, she wouldn't tell me. I was about ready to cry myself.

The nice cop told me, since this was their first offense and they were sixteen years old, that they could go through a program with community hours and drug education and have it taken off their records when they finished. He confided in me that his son had made some similar mistakes when he was younger.

It was so refreshing to actually meet a nice cop. The girls did their community hours at an animal shelter and swore to be good from then on. It really scared them. I was more suspicious of Abigail and her friends after that. I had a friend who worked at the courthouse where the program the girls had to complete was. She helped me get Abigail's charge expunged.

My First Heart Fling after Ted

ONE OF MY GIRL FRIENDS WAS GOOD friends with another doctor in town, Carlos. She said she wanted to get us together. I told her I wasn't real sure about it. I had taken the boys to him a few times; and he was very professional, friendly, and always busy. I finally agreed.

He called me up one night and asked me to go to dinner with him and another couple on the weekend. I said yes, and we had a lot of fun together. I really started to like him. He was so different from anyone else that I had gone out with and was my first real date since Ted had died. He was Hispanic, and sometimes I couldn't understand what he was saying. I would laugh and tell him to slow down so I could understand him.

One night, we went to a bar with the same couple. It was a rather quiet bar, and while we were eating, about seven or eight of his younger friends all rode up on motorcycles. They were yelling back and forth to one another and to Carlos in Spanish. They all came in, and he bought them drinks.

What was previously a quiet little bar was now a loud, crazy Spanish fiesta. I was a little embarrassed at first because I knew some of the other people there, and everyone was staring at us and Carlos's friends. We were having so much fun, though, that I just enjoyed myself. My old party girl side was coming out.

I was working nights again at a nursing home part time, and Carlos would text me when I was at work. He would always tell me he was thinking of me. He was so romantic. I would text him back on my breaks. One night, I was working the three-to-eleven shift when he texted me and asked me to go over to his place after work, and we could give each other back rubs. We hadn't slept together or even seen each other naked, so I was really hesitant about going over there.

He always took a sleeping pill because he had difficulty sleeping, and I told him he would probably be asleep by the time I got off work. He said he would wait up for me and not take his sleeping pill. He texted me at about ten thirty and said he was falling asleep, and he would call me tomorrow. I was relieved not to have to go over there. I was concerned that we might end up in bed together, and I didn't want that to happen.

Carlos was arrested that morning. He had been selling narcotics scripts to undercover agents, who turned him in because he wasn't examining them. They had been doing an investigation on him, and I knew absolutely nothing about it. I might have been there when he was arrested if he hadn't fallen asleep. My guardian angels were working overtime for me and saved me from what could have been a very embarrassing and bad situation.

I saw his picture on the front page of our local newspaper. My heart sank. It was a picture of him being put in the police car. I guess he didn't know the sheriff well enough to keep it out of the news, like the other family had with their son and the cocaine in the uncle's car trunk.

Yes, he was wrong in what he was doing, and a side of me was very angry that he was part of a group of doctors who were selling narcotics scripts. After all I had been through with the boys and Ted, it hit too close to my heart.

He did have a good side, though. I had a friend who had a mentally challenged brother, and Carlos would make house calls to see him. He was the only doctor the kid trusted because he was so nice to him. All of Carlos's patients loved him because he was so caring and gave them good care. He was also very smart.

My thought was that Carlos was messed up emotionally because his ex-wife was a super witch. She had been living with another man, a carpenter she met while he was working at their house. They were still married, and Carlos was paying the bills while the boyfriend lived in his house. I never understood why he let her get away with that for three years. Carlos was living on the second floor of his office building. He told me he had intentionally married an unattractive woman, thinking that she wouldn't cheat on him. She definitely was not attractive in any way. He used to tell me I was his trophy.

Faye, his ex, was so mean. She sold his Porsche for a lot less than it was worth and had a garage sale at his office before it was sold. She sold everything that was in his office and some of his personal belongings from the house without telling him while he was out of town, waiting for his court case.

Carlos had a wealthy brother down south, who got the best lawyers for him and spent a million dollars defending him. He ended up spending two years in jail and, of course, lost his license. He taught some of the inmates so that they could get their GEDs. When he got out, his brother bought him a condo and had him doing research for him.

He texted me when he got out and wanted to get together again. I told him we were too far away from each other. He wasn't good for me, even though I really liked him. I'm sure he has plenty of girlfriends to choose from down south.

A rumor started circulating, which one of my friends told me about. Apparently, I was giving Carlos the best blow jobs ever. I was fuming when I heard that, and when I saw Faye, his ex, in the gym, I confronted her about the rumor. I told her I didn't appreciate her lying about me and since I had never seen Carlos naked, it would have been difficult to give him a blow job. She just looked at me and told me that her girlfriends had told her about it. Just one more reminder to me of what a small-town mentality Water City had. I have wondered if maybe Carlos had started the rumor himself to make his soon to be ex-wife jealous.

Funny how things worked out sometimes. When Carlos's office building came up for sale, Dr. Melvin Toste and his wife, Greeda, immediately snatched it up. It was newer and bigger than Ted's office. They finally sold the old office and then bought another one. They never could be happy with what they had and always wanted more as I mentioned before. One of his nurses told me that Melvin was always working and didn't get to see his kids much.

Life was going smoothly with Mark out West in school and Adam living in the sober living apartments. The girls were good, and I finally started to relax a little more.

I decided to have a laser done on my face by my plastic surgeon, Dr. McLovin. He was such a knowledgeable and friendly guy. He reminded me of a teddy bear, although he told me he was working out more and wanted to build more muscle. I told him not to get messed up in the steroid world. He said, "No way."

I had already had a full face-lift ten years before by his senior partner, who had just retired. Dr. McLovin took over. I got another boob job, a tummy tuck to get rid of the little baby fat from having four children, a mini-face-lift, and fillers. I've always kept myself physically fit, but because of all the sun from my younger years, I felt like I needed some extra help with my face also. He made my lips fuller, and I really liked them. I went home to recuperate and relax.

Mark's Fall

I HAD BEEN HOME RECUPERATING FOR ABOUT a week, and then I got a call from Adam. He sounded frantic as he told me that Mark had called him, told him he had taken some magic mushrooms, and was freaking out on the top of a mountain he was hiking. Adam said he was talking to him, and then all of a sudden, he couldn't hear him anymore. We were both very concerned, and I told Adam that I would find out more information and call him back.

I started praying to God to please cover Mark with the blood of Jesus and save him again. I decided I would call Gwen, the receptionist at Mark's apartment complex. I had met her when I went out to Colorado to help Mark find his apartment. She told me she had heard something on the radio but didn't think it was Mark. She told me she would send out her maintenance man, Jim, to try to find him. She didn't tell me at that time what she had heard.

After waiting for several long hours, Gwen called me back. She said that Jim found Mark in the hospital. Then she told me what she had heard on the radio and that it was also on the news on television.

Mark said he had taken some mushrooms ten hours before and went hiking up the mountain by himself. I had told him before he even started hiking to never go by himself, but of course, he never listened to me. I was just his mother. Apparently, it was not that uncommon for people who lived out of state to fall down the mountains or get lost.

When he had called Adam, he was high from the hallucinogen, and there was another hiker up there. He noticed that Mark was acting kind of weird. Mark lost his balance and fell two hundred feet down the mountain. There were several rescue teams called to help him, and they took him to the hospital. He told me he had lost consciousness when he first landed and then fell a second time once he was more aware.

He ended up going into surgery for nine broken bones in his foot and ankle and multiple abrasions all over his body. He also had to have a plastic surgeon sew part of his ear back on. I knew without a doubt that God and His angels saved Mark again. The chances of him surviving that fall were very slim, and thank God there was another hiker on the mountain who saw Mark fall and called for rescue. Mark could have died right there on the mountain with no one even knowing he was there.

The doctors told Mark that anyone who had a traumatic brain injury was going to have temporary brain damage. They told him it almost always comes back, but some people take longer than others. He had to have a speech therapist work with him to make sure that he would be well enough mentally to go back to school the next semester. This really hurt his ego because he had always been a good student, even while taking heroin. As I said, there are functioning abusers who can still do what they normally do, and no one would even know they are doing drugs. That was the way Ted was also.

Mark had several friends who visited him every day in the hospital. Jim said he didn't recognize him at first because of all the bandages all over him. He had plenty of attention since everyone in Colorado heard about it on the news. When Mark asked me to fly out there immediately, I told him that it would be better to wait until he got home. He had all the nurses and doctors right there in the hospital.

After he was released, I flew out there to check out his situation. Of course, his apartment was a mess, and he had about six loads of dirty laundry. He couldn't walk without crutches, and then only for emergencies. Most of the time, he had to be in a wheelchair. I felt kind of sorry for him, but it was his own fault. I cooked for him, cleaned up his apartment, and did his dirty laundry.

While I was there, I got to meet his home health nurses who did his wound care, and they showed me how to do it also. I met his physical therapist and speech therapist. I was impressed that they all came to his apartment and was very thankful that they did. It was difficult for Mark to get in and out of his apartment.

He dropped out of school for a semester but thankfully got back in for the next semester with no issues, and they reimbursed him his money. He said he had left Florida to get away from the drugs. The pill mills were being cracked down on, and doctors were being arrested right and left. The fact that he did the mushrooms really ticked me off, but I thanked God that he was still alive.

I told Mark that God obviously saved him for a reason, and he needed to figure out what God's purpose was for his life. He had been saved multiple times when he should have died. I think he was finally beginning to understand what I had been trying to get him to realize for so long.

I have learned through nursing and having to deal with sickness and the drug world that life is very fragile. We are not guaranteed tomorrow. Thank God for every day that we and our loved ones are alive and well. I live moment to moment trying my best to trust Him with everything.

After I left to come home, Mark got his friends to drive him around and girl friends to cook and clean for him. Eventually, he started using a walking boot and slowly healed. His torn earlobe was not even noticeable. Emotionally, he was pretty beat up, though, and I just prayed that he learned his lesson from this.

He had been attending a church with mostly young people. I was happy about that, until he told me that they all abandoned him as friends when they found out what had happened. I was really angry at first, but then I remembered that people are often afraid of what they don't understand and tend to judge others as has happened in our past before.

I told Mark to just forgive them and find another group of friends who were more open to forgiveness. I did take one of his friends from church out to dinner with Mark. He was the only one who stuck by him. He actually witnessed to students on campus. His name was Rodney, and he was an attractive young man with long curly blond hair and a beard. He was the one who told me that many people had fallen down the mountains, and several were killed. Mostly, they were people who weren't used to climbing the mountains, like people out of state.

It was nice to get home, but it was so beautiful in Colorado in a completely different way from Florida. God's beauty is everywhere. Staying there with Mark brought back a lot of good memories of when I went to school there many years ago. It was much quainter before, though.

Since marijuana was legal there both medicinally and recreationally, Colorado was booming. There was construction everywhere because so many people were moving in. Mark and I went to a dispensary, and the people there looked like everyday people, not a bunch of long-haired potheads, like so many people had a stereotype of. Everyone was polite and professional.

I would have liked to go to a medical dispensary. I had voted yes for medical marijuana in Florida, especially since I had seen it help my cancer patients years ago. If I had a child who was having multiple seizures every day and knew that marijuana helped reduce the amount of seizures, I would have taken my child out there. Also, it was supposed to help glaucoma, and my sweet daddy eventually went blind, and they attributed it to senile glaucoma. Perhaps it would have helped him also.

Since I had more free time now, I decided to go back to work and try something different. I took some online courses to get qualified to teach VPK (voluntary prekindergarten). I always loved kids, and there was an opening at a church nearby. Since my own kids were older now, I looked forward to being with four-year-olds again. I got a job as a teacher's assistant, which I really wanted, and loved it. The children were so sweet, and I got to wear my regular clothes instead of a nursing uniform. I tried to wear clothes and jewelry that the kids would like.

The main teacher was young enough to be my daughter. We had nothing in common, but I tried to be her friend. She was overweight, talked in a monotone, and hardly ever smiled. I felt sorry for her, though, because her baby died in her arms right after it was born. Thankfully, she got pregnant later because she didn't have any other children.

The woman supervisor was very stern, was divorced from a pastor, and never had children. Needless to say, we had nothing in common either. I really didn't like the way she treated some of the children there.

I became friends with two of the other girls who worked with the two- and three-year-olds. They both brought me welcome gifts since I was the newest teacher there, and I immediately liked both of them.

The kids and I got along great, and I loved being with them. There was one beautiful little redheaded boy who was the challenge of the class. He had a difficult time sitting still, and his parents had just gone through a divorce. He preferred being with me over the younger head teacher. I also knew his mom from the gym. I think the teacher was a little jealous of me and how well I got along with the kids and the parents. I could relate with the parents better because we all had children, and the teacher and the supervisor didn't.

One day, we had a cop come to visit the class. He was coming to talk about strangers. He told the kids not to open the door to someone you didn't know or go anywhere with someone you didn't know. He talked about several other situations, and I agreed with what his message was to the kids.

After the talk was finished, he told us he was going to take us out to see his truck. I assumed it would be a police car or truck. They drove so many different kinds of vehicles now, especially unidentified ones. When we got outside, a big shiny black truck was in the parking lot. He proceeded to tell the four-year-olds that the truck used to be a drug dealer's truck, but now it was his. I was livid.

He was supposed to come to talk about how to handle situations with strangers, not glamorize how beautiful the drug dealer's truck was. I thought it was very inappropriate, especially with these little four-year-olds' impressionable minds. They might think it would be cool to have a truck like that and that selling drugs would be a way to get one.

Then he turned on the loud speakers in the truck and had all the kids climb through the truck and dance to the music. I didn't dance but quietly watched the kids as they did. I didn't approve of the whole situation and felt like it was my right not to dance, especially at a church preschool, around a drug dealer's truck.

The unattractive fat cop got his ego bent out of shape, and when I didn't dance, he mentioned it to the supervisor on the way back to the preschool classroom. Wilma, the supervisor, called me into her office after school and told me it was very rude of me not to dance with the kids, since the policeman was considered a visitor. I couldn't believe she told me that, and I told her that it was my personal right not to dance, and I didn't approve of him talking about drug dealers to four-year-olds. I didn't let her try to intimidate me.

Wilma came into my classroom after school a few days later and asked me if I would be interested in working with the two-year-olds. She said I was so nurturing that I might be a better fit with the younger children because I was too nice to the four-year-olds. I really didn't want to change diapers and babysit all day, so I told her I wasn't interested. Then she told me that she had another person to take my place. I quit and told her how surprised I was that she felt that way. I was sure that the teacher and she just didn't understand how to treat children because they never had children of their own.

I thought about going to the minister, but that would have put him in the middle. He had already told me how happy he was to have me working there. The janitor and I had become friends, and he told me he had seen several good teachers leave and that I wasn't the only one treated unfairly. He also told me he had seen some of the children mistreated. I knew I had made the right decision to leave.

I called the police department and asked them to talk to the supervisor. I told them about the cop who came to the preschool and glamorized the drug dealer's truck. It just so happened that I knew the supervisor on duty. He had helped me with Adam's truck when he had it impounded when he got in trouble with Hellen. He said he would talk to the officer, and he agreed with me that he had been inappropriate.

I found out later from one of the teachers I liked at the preschool that Wilma had been asked to leave the school. Also, the teacher of the VPK had been replaced by one of the other teachers that I liked. Here was another example of "what goes around comes around."

I really missed being with the kids. One day, when I was at the gym, the dad of two the preschoolers came up to me and told me how much his twins and the rest of the people at the preschool missed me there. He said I was one of the few who would actually talk to the parents and that his twins really liked me. They were beautiful and well-behaved little girls. He made my day when he told me that.

The Assisted-Living Experience

I TOOK A BREAK FOR A WHILE and decided I would get back into the nursing world again. I applied for a part-time position at an assisted-living facility, which had an ad in the local newspaper. The nurse that hired me was really nice, and we hit it off immediately. She hired me for the 7:00 a.m.–2:00 p.m. shift with no weekends. I only worked two days a week. It was a perfect schedule for me. I certainly didn't want to work in a hospital, so I thought this would be a good experience for me.

Abigail was still in high school and had a new boyfriend. Melissa was still living at home but worked part time as a bartender at night. I didn't want Abigail at home with her boyfriend if no one else was there. Melissa and I had an agreement that she would watch Abigail while I was at work, in case I was running a little late.

I got hired for working in the lockdown unit with the memory loss unit. This was another way of referring to the residents with Alzheimer's and dementia. They were just like little two-year-olds and wanted to follow me wherever I went. Most of the residents were very sweet and just wanted somebody to be nice to them. Two of my mother's friends from my childhood were residents there. It made me sad to see them there because I knew them when they were so active and independent. My mom was becoming more and more like them.

It was a nice facility. It was called the Refuge. I liked the name; it was very calming. The decor was pretty; and they had a coffee shop, an ice cream parlor, and a beauty salon. The food was good, and I liked all the people I worked with. I learned how to give meds from a computer and basically really liked my job.

We had thought about putting my mom and dad in there, but since my dad was blind, we decided to keep the 24/7 caretakers at their home. The caretakers were good with my parents, and they got individualized attention. Many older children are taking care of their aging parents in some capacity, be it at their homes or at a facility. If the funds aren't there, they have to make arrangements to have family members take care of them, and it can be very stressful. I am already praying that I will always be independent and healthy and just go in my sleep to be with the Lord.

While I was working at the Refuge, they made some changes without telling the nurses ahead of time. The nurse who hired me had left because she wanted to go back to school and have a baby. They changed my shift to 2:00 p.m. to 8:00 p.m. They also made me supervisor. That meant I had to do all the breathing treatments and diabetic care and take care of emergencies and petty situations, which the other techs could have easily taken care of. I never got out when I was supposed to because it was impossible to do a thorough job on my lockdown unit and then have to help everybody else. It took thirty minutes to commute to work, and I wasn't getting home till nine thirty or ten at night.

Abigail had met her boyfriend at the private school she had attended since first grade. He was new at the school and was the star basketball player on the school team. He also had received three countywide awards. I assumed he was on a "scholarship," but I was not sure. We enjoyed watching him play with all his fancy moves.

He seemed like a nice-enough guy, but I wasn't sure about him at first. Abigail always had lots of girl friends and guy friends over to the house. He was her first real boyfriend. His name was Jamal. I asked Abigail about his family, and she told me that his father was black and a truck driver. He didn't marry the mom, and they had another little girl, about ten years old. She was adorable. The father would have affairs and leave the family and then come back home again when the affair was over. It made me angry, especially after everything I had gone through with Ted. I really didn't want Abigail hanging around that kind of atmosphere. Our family had already been through more than enough drama.

I met Jamal's mom at school at one of the basketball games. She was a pretty white blonde, a little overweight but worked and was very pleasant. I couldn't understand why she would keep taking Jamal's dad back but assumed it was because of her kids. That was the reason I had stayed with Ted. I just kept my mouth shut and hoped that Jamal and Abigail would end up miles apart, going to different colleges.

Jamal would come over to our house and ride our jet ski like a maniac. I had told him and Abigail that Jamal could not drive the jet ski by himself. He was not insured, and Abigail had to drive or at least be with him. He didn't listen to me. I would look out the window, and he would be riding by himself, with Abigail sitting on the dock. It made me start resenting him.

I had told them that Melissa had been in a jet ski accident, and she ended up with three broken ribs and a punctured lung. She had let one of her friends drive it, and then Melissa fell off because her friend turned too fast. I prayed that Melissa would heal quickly, and she was at the gym three days later. I couldn't believe it. God had certainly had His angels around her then. The ER bill was $11,000. I told Jamal and Abigail that I didn't want to go through that again.

I ended up paying $1,650 to have the jet ski fixed after Jamal drove it. I started feeling like he was using Abigail, and I really didn't want them together alone at the house. Abigail was beautiful and smart and well-liked by her peers. She and Jamal were elected prom queen and king. I was excited for her.

Even though I liked my job, I had to quit. Abigail was much more important to me than my job. Now I could be home at night, and if Jamal was there, I was there also. Melissa liked being able to do what she wanted without babysitting her little sister.

They had told me at the assisted living that I was paying too much attention to the residents and that I needed to speed things up. That just wasn't my kind of nursing, so I knew I really didn't belong there. The director of the Refuge wasn't even a medical person. He had been a manager at a grocery store. How could he possibly relate to medical issues? When I was told I was paying too much attention to the residents, it reminded me of when I was told I was too nice to the VPK kids. What is this world coming to when you are told you are too nice to four-year-olds and Alzheimer's residents? There is something wrong there.

I saw one of my supervisors later after I quit. She told me that two nurses who were hired after me quit on the spot and didn't last but a few days. I had stayed about five months and at least gave my two weeks' notice. Also, one of the other nursing administrators quit. I knew then that I had definitely made the right decision. Abigail and Jamal continued to see each other, but at least I was home.

Disappointment, Forgiveness, and Saying Good-Bye

GRADUATION DAY ARRIVED, AND ABIGAIL GOT ACCEPTED to a well-established private college with a partial scholarship. Some of her close friends got accepted there also, and it was only two hours away. Jamal got a four-year fully paid basketball scholarship to a college in the Northwest. It would be a great opportunity for him and Abigail, and he would be at far ends of the United States. I was happy about this.

Unfortunately, he couldn't pass the preadmission test and couldn't keep the scholarship. Abigail told me he had planned on helping his father load his truck or become a truck driver like his father. This bothered me because Abigail had already told me that Jamal's father had girlfriends. A friend of mine had told me that there were prostitutes who hung out at the truck stops, who were called lot lizards. I really didn't want Jamal being exposed to that lifestyle and following in his father's footsteps. I was so disappointed, but he said that he tried the test twice. He said that if he had gone to Holy Shepherd, the private school, he probably would have done better. He was only there his senior year. In a way, I understood what he was saying. I told him he could at least go to a junior college and play basketball there.

Now I really didn't want Abigail with him. It wasn't that I didn't like him personally; I just felt like he lacked motivation. My dad had been a doctor, and I watched how Ted had studied so hard all the way through medical school and internship and then residency. All I had asked of my own children was to at least get a college education. I told my kids and Jamal that my dad had told me years ago that the one thing his wealthiest patients wished they had done was to get a college degree. It was something to fall back on if needed, and no one could ever take it away from you. However, if you were stupid enough to do something illegal, you could have your license taken away from you.

The more negative things I said about Jamal not going to school or having a decent job, the more it pushed her away. Even though all my friends and her siblings agreed with me, I had to learn to keep my mouth shut. I told her not to spend money on him after I realized she was paying for his dinner several times when they went out. I told her that her trust money was for her and school, not Jamal. I changed her account at the bank so I could keep track of each transaction she was making with her debit card.

She got angry with me and probably frustrated and told me I couldn't tell her what to do anymore since she was in college. I reminded her that I was in control of her trust money, and Ted's will said I didn't have to give her any money till she was twenty-five years old. I reminded her that I thought her father would definitely have agreed with me about Jamal.

Thank God we had put her on birth control pills earlier for her migraine headaches before she was seeing Jamal. She had been taking mega doses of a medicine for migraines, and her doctor also got migraines. She thought it would be a good idea to have Abigail take the birth control pills to see if they would help. Little did I know that they would definitely help when she was with Jamal. I think one of the reasons Abigail was still with Jamal was because he was her first real physical love. I remembered how stupid I was when I was young, and Abigail asked me if I would rather see her get drunk, like a lot of the girls at college, and end up with a bunch of different guys. I didn't know what to say. I just told her neither scenario was a good one.

I have gotten to the point that I put all my concerns into God's hands about all my children's lives and mine. I give the best advice I can and pray that God gives me wisdom. I pray that each of my children are Christ followers and glorify God. I wish that I had been wiser when I was younger, so I understand how poor decisions can be made.

I got a huge surprise one day. Our home phone rang, and I hardly ever answered it because it was usually solicitors. My friends called me on my cell. I looked at the name that came up on my phone and couldn't believe it. It was Landon, my first husband, whom I hadn't seen for twenty-five years. I answered the phone, and Landon said he had gotten my phone number when they were doing a background check on him for a new job. He said he still loved me and wanted to be my lover again. That kind of made me uneasy. I told him I wasn't looking for a lover, but a friend would be nice.

We talked for about an hour, and it was so nice to hear his voice. I had actually tried to find out where he was to apologize for being such a slut when I was married to him. I apologized to him then, and he said he forgave me. He said we were both different people now, and he knew that he suffered from post-traumatic stress syndrome from the Vietnam War. I told him that I had finally grown up when I had kids, and attention from the opposite sex just fed my ego, but I wasn't interested in having affairs.

I felt like a heavy burden had been lifted off my shoulders and my heart. I had felt bad for so long about my past behavior with men. With God's and Landon's forgiveness, I felt like I had a new freedom about myself. We talked about possibly meeting halfway and getting together for old time's sake. I really do want to see him, but he lives in a different state, and I still remember how he scared me sometimes with his jealousy. He was is a good person, though, and didn't do drugs and hardly ever drank. He was a hard worker, and we had fun together. Sometimes I think it would be nice to have him here with me, but I will see what God has planned.

My sweet daddy started getting worse physically; and every time I would go to visit him, it just made me so sad to see him blind, deaf, and unable to walk. He would not have wanted to be like that. He had spent most of his life taking care of sick and dying people, and I knew he would be going to heaven. I was with him the night he passed, and it reminded me of the first patient I saw take her last breath when I was a new nurse in the hospital. At least now he can dance with the angels and his twin sister and siblings.

We had daddy cremated, and Brad, my brother, and I got his ashes and spread them out in the fields where he used to take us quail and dove hunting when we were younger. I loved those times with my dad because he worked such crazy doctor's hours that I didn't get to spend a whole lot of time with him. The owner of the ranch and his wife helped us. He had huge respect for my dad and asked if he could be part of the celebration. I knew in my heart that this was what Dad would have wanted us to do. The rest of his ashes were spread at the designated area at his church where I grew up in. In fact, one of his thirteen-year-old patients had her ashes spread there too. She had died of juvenile diabetes many years ago and was the sister of a friend of mine.

My mom really missed him at first. She would go around the house looking for him. She was in and out of reality with the Alzheimer's and most of the time didn't know who I was. It made me sad to see her like that, but I knew her caretakers were good to her. She didn't do much but watch television and look at the newspaper. I didn't know if she could really read it or not. Brad and I have thought about putting her in an assisted living, where she would have more stimulation, but we would see what God has planned.

Our Family Journeys Continue

I THOUGHT ABOUT SELLING OUR HOUSE, BUT the panoramic view of the lake is so beautiful. With most of the kids gone, it is a pretty big house for just me. I am just waiting to see what Melissa and Abigail will end up doing next year. Empty-nest syndrome is real.

Mark is staying in Colorado for a while. He just finished his last two classes and wanted to take a break. He got a new job at a marijuana dispensary and grow house. He is learning all about how to grow marijuana and which diseases or symptoms would be best helped by specific species or strains. I prayed about him getting this job before he got it. He was good friends with the son of the owner. They met at the gym. He loved his job and worked overtime, six days a week. I was happy that he was also making his own money, but I told him it would be nice if he could at least take one class at night toward his bachelor degree. He wanted to learn as much as possible so he could open his own place when people got wiser and more informed and saw that medical marijuana really helped people. The government just made so much money on the pharmaceutical business. He is now looking for a house to grow his own plants. He got his legal medical marijuana grower's license that allows him to grow 99 plants legally for others. Now he can be his own boss. He has also gotten into super fit physical condition and is a fitness model.

Adam was in north Florida, going to college, or so I thought. He talked about being a lawyer, but that was several years away. I just prayed for him to finish school and find a job he was happy with. I got another shock when I found out he wasn't even in school and was doing heroin for the past few months with one of his roommates. He had hidden his use from his other roommate and his girlfriend as well. I ended up taking him to another rehab in Colorado and now he is living out there with Mark. I have told Mark it is his job to watch over his little brother and be his hero. I put them in God's hands and pray for them 24/7.

Melissa has changed her major from Nutrition to Nursing. I am very happy about this. Two of her best friends are nurses and I'm sure they have influenced her in a good way.

Abigail said she and several of her friends didn't like the smaller private college she went to her first semester. Since it was so expensive, I told her she didn't have to stay. She attended a junior college closer to where Jamal lives, but my prayers have been answered. Jamal and Abigail are no longer together and I am very happy about this. I pray that he gets motivated and makes something out of his life, but not with Abigail.

I did something kind of risky a few months ago. I stupidly joined a dating service where they interview each candidate personally and have "matchmakers" put you together. They also do a background check on everyone. I joined on-line after I took my sleeping pill, which I take because I sleep with two midgets that snore—my dogs. They are so loud that I can't sleep, and they won't sleep anywhere else. Anyway, after I take my sleeping pill, I need to go straight to bed, or I do stupid things.

I had prayed that God would put the right people in my pathway to interview me. My interviewer was a pretty twenty-seven-year-old, whose mother was a pastor. We got friendly, and she told me her biological father was a jerk; and when he died, her stepfather, who was very wealthy, adopted her. She said she was only working there because she wanted to help people. I believed her.

She was very naive about drugs, and I found it very refreshing. She reminded me of how I had been before I had to deal with the drug world with my own family. I told her I wasn't 100 percent sure I wanted to do this, and she said that I wasn't getting any younger, and now was the best time. My own friend down the street had told me the same thing. I started to think that maybe I should give it a try, and God would lead me. I prayed that something good would happen.

I told Toni, my interviewer, that I wanted a Christian man who was physically fit and worked out, intelligent, friendly, and close to my age. I felt like I had those qualities, so it was fair to ask for the same. Ted had all those qualities when I first met him, only he was five years younger, and he had pursued me. I will have to admit that I was very skeptical of all men now. I was also thinking that he would have to be very patient with my boys, and my kids would be so surprised if I actually started dating someone.

I trusted Toni and her company to do me right, so I paid a good amount of money to do this. My first date was at a local restaurant. He was sitting at the bar, waiting for me. We somehow knew that we were each other's date. He was very nice and easy to talk to. He was a professor and had traveled the world. In the middle of our conversation, he asked me if I was a Christian because he could tell by the way I was talking. I said, "Yes, and you are also, right?" He said no, that he was Buddhist. We both were annoyed with the dating company for overlooking this very important request. We were very pleasant with each other and decided to just cut the date off short. I was ticked off, and so was he. He said he had been on three dates already, and I was the first one he liked.

I called the service the next business day and told them I didn't appreciate them setting me up with a Buddhist. It really hit home with me because Ted and Isabel had been reading Buddhist books together. The woman I talked to said they could only go by what the client told them, and he had not mentioned that he was Buddhist. I told her I wanted my money back, but she said I had signed a contract for fourteen dates, and they would do their best to find me a better match. I would give them another chance and pray that God would lead His choice to the agency. I talked to my lawyer about possibly getting out of the contract, but he said it wouldn't be worth it. Then he told me that he had recently gotten a divorce. I was shocked. He seemed like the perfect man!

The girls and I went to visit Mark and Adam. We had fun climbing the mountains and seeing the leaves turn their beautiful colors. It was hard to believe that, just a year before, Mark had fallen down the same mountain and nearly killed himself. The Lord works in mysterious ways. I praise Him for His favor on our family.

I decided to get another mini-face-lift from my plastic surgeon, Dr. McLovin. When I saw the anesthesiologist, I about flipped out. He had a bandana on his head and earrings in both earlobes. I was trying to grow older gracefully, but God and I were still working on this.

I've been thinking about older age recently. I guess because, after being a nurse now for almost forty years, I have seen so much. My mom and dad's health issues have made me think that people are living too long. When Jesus walked the earth, we didn't have all these medicines and tests that we have now. People just died. I have changed my will to have no funeral and my ashes to be spread at the church with my dad's—ashes to ashes, dust to dust. I also want some of them spread over the Rocky Mountains or the lake I lived on. Brad and I were supposed to each inherit a million dollars. I would much rather have my parents travel the world healthy and vibrant and inherit nothing. I don't want any heroics either, and hopefully, marijuana would be legal when it is my time to go in my sleep.

On a lighter note, my ninety-five-year-old mother-in-law is still ticking along. God has worked such a miracle with our relationship. We are friends, and she told me that I am one of her best friends. Years ago, she hated me, and prayer changed everything. She is living in an assisted-living facility near her daughter, my sister-in-law. We are friends also. Anthony, my brother-in-law who smashed my face, found a place to live on his own. He has cut down on his drinking and appears healthier. I pray that he gets closer to God.

I haven't heard anything new about Isabel, except that she went to church on Christmas Eve. I told my friend who saw her that there was hope for everyone. She said she was only there to be seen by her ex-friends.

My life has brought me through a journey of peaks and valleys. Through it all, God, Jesus, and the Holy Spirit have gotten me through it. They say you have to be broken before you can truly realize the power of God. Well, I have definitely been broken, but I have come back much stronger with more faith to conquer the future with God's love and protection around me and my children. We claim the generational blessing.

I wrote this book about my journey praying that it would help at least one person get closer to our Lord. I pray that you will see that you can't make it on your own. Jesus is my best friend. He is always with me and loves me just the way I am, even after all the sins I have committed. He loves you too. Remember, though, that the closer you get to the Lord, expect the devil to tempt you more because he doesn't want you to be a Christ follower. He wants you to follow him instead. Just believe, make good decisions, and stay strong. The rest of your journey awaits you.

CPSIA information can be obtained
at www.ICGtesting.com
Printed in the USA
FSOW02n0125120217
30675FS